P9-CQW-346

WITHDRAWN
TEMPLE PUBLIC LIBRARY

TEMPLE PUBLIC LIBRARY
100 West Adams Avenue
Temple, Texas 76501

HIS VIRGIN
MISTRESS

HIS VIRGIN MISTRESS

BY

ANNE MATHER

LP
F
M 427hi

MILLS & BOON®

26.95

All the characters in this book have no existence outside the imagination of the author, and have no relation whatsoever to anyone bearing the same name or names. They are not even distantly inspired by any individual known or unknown to the author, and all the incidents are pure invention.

All Rights Reserved including the right of reproduction in whole or in part in any form. This edition is published by arrangement with Harlequin Enterprises II B.V. The text of this publication or any part thereof may not be reproduced or transmitted in any form or by any means, electronic or mechanical, including photocopying, recording, storage in an information retrieval system, or otherwise, without the written permission of the publisher.

MILLS & BOON and
MILLS & BOON with the Rose Device
are registered trademarks of the publisher.

First published in Great Britain 2002
Large Print edition 2003
Harlequin Mills & Boon Limited,
Eton House, 18-24 Paradise Road,
Richmond, Surrey TW9 1SR

© Anne Mather 2002

ISBN 0 263 17869 2

Set in Times Roman 15½ on 17 pt.
16-0103-58060

Printed and bound in Great Britain
by Antony Rowe Ltd, Chippenham, Wiltshire

CHAPTER ONE

'Is THAT her?'

'Yes, sir.' Spiro Stavros gave his employer a faintly sardonic look. 'Not exactly what you'd anticipated, is she?'

Demetrios Kastro arched a dismissive brow. As yet his arrival had not been noticed, and he was able to look across the crowded salon to where his father and his companion were standing without being observed. They were surrounded by the guests who had been invited to welcome the old man back to Theapolis, and Demetri watched with a tightening of his jawline as his father put a possessive arm about the woman's shoulders.

'Perhaps not,' he conceded at last, aware that Spiro knew exactly what he was thinking. He had expected her to be younger. A 'blonde bimbo' was how she had been described to him by his sister, and because it was what he had wanted to hear he had believed her. But the woman his father had adopted as his mistress didn't look like a bimbo. There was intelligence as well as beauty in the high-cheekboned face, with its wide-set eyes and mobile mouth, and, although she was

5

undoubtedly a blonde, she wore her hair drawn up into a severe knot that, whatever its purpose, tended to draw attention to the slender column of her neck. 'She is certainly older than I had imagined.'

'And more sophisticated?' suggested Spiro drily. 'I have the feeling she is not going to be as easy to get rid of as you thought.'

Demetri cast his assistant a dark look. 'You think not?' He was cynical. 'In my experience, my friend, everyone has their price. Man or woman. It makes no difference. If the rewards are great enough, they all succumb.'

Spiro's snort was disbelieving. 'Do you include me in that assessment?'

Demetri sighed. 'We were not talking about you, Spiro.'

'That does not answer my question.'

'All right.' Demetri scowled. 'I would hope not. I consider you my friend as well as my assistant. But few people are as scrupulous, Spiro. You know that.'

'Not all women are like Athenee, Demetri,' the other man reminded him gently. Then, aware that he was in danger of overstepping the mark, he added, 'I suppose I must consider myself honoured.' He grimaced. 'So? What are you going to do now?'

'Now?' Demetri's dark, tanned features smoothed themselves into an urbane mask. 'Why, now I am going to announce my arrival to my father, and ask to be introduced to the delightful Kiria Manning.'

Spiro's mouth compressed and, taking a chance, he put a detaining hand on Demetri's sleeve. 'Be careful,' he said, risking a rebuff. But although his hand was shaken off, Demetri merely gave him a mocking smile.

'Am I not always?' he enquired, loosening the button on the jacket of his dark blue silk suit. 'Calm yourself, Spiro. I am not likely to show my hand so early in the game.'

Nevertheless, as Demetri made his way across the room he was aware of an intense feeling of irritation. Dammit, his father had only been out of hospital for a few weeks; weeks that he had spent in London, ostensibly to avoid the blistering heat of Theapolis in mid-summer. The old man had been ill; seriously ill. In God's name, when had he found the time to meet this woman, let alone become intimate with her?

He would find out. Offering a word of greeting here, an acknowledgement of welcome there, he gradually covered the space dividing him from Constantine Kastro and his mistress. What was her name? Manning, yes. But what was her first name? Demetri frowned, thinking. Joanna! That was it. Joanna Manning. Was it her real name? If so, it was elegant, just like the woman herself.

'Do not tell me that frown is because you are sad to see me back, Demetri.'

His father's chiding words—spoken in English for the woman's benefit, Demetri assumed—were delivered in a mocking tone. Demetri realised he was allowing too much of his feelings to show in his face and he hastily schooled his features. Then, finding a polite smile, he shook the old man's hand and submitted to the customary embrace with genuine warmth.

'Forgive me, Papa,' he said disarmingly, and no one could tell from his expression that he was anything but delighted with the present situation. 'Naturally, I am relieved your physicians consider you well enough to return to us at last.'

Constantine looked less than pleased now, his narrow features mirroring his discontent. 'I am not an invalid, Demetri,' he declared irritably, even though his wasted body belied the fact. 'The doctors have given me a clean bill of health, and I do not appreciate you behaving as if I had only just got out of hospital.'

Demetri made no response to this. Instead, his eyes moved to the woman standing at his father's side, and, because they were surrounded by interested spectators, Constantine was obliged to introduce his companion to his son.

'My dear,' he said and Demetri stiffened at the implied intimacy in the term. 'Allow me to present my son to you. Demetrios: this is Joanna. Joanna Manning. My—my friend.'

'How do you do?'

The woman didn't make the mistake of calling him by his first name and Demetri's thin lips stretched into a tight smile. 'It is my pleasure to meet you, Kiria Manning,' he responded politely. 'I trust you are not finding our weather too trying for your English tastes?'

'On the contrary.' Despite the faint film of perspiration on her upper lip, she denied it. 'I love the heat. It's so—sensual.'

Sensual?

Demetri had to work hard to prevent himself from showing his incredulity. He had heard his father was besotted by the woman, but he hadn't expected her to disconcert him. And why was she watching him with that air of amused speculation? She was taller than most of the women of his acquaintance—easily five feet eight or nine—and, although he was still almost a head taller than she was, she didn't have to tilt her head too far to look up at him. If he hadn't known better he'd have wondered if she wasn't deliberately trying to irritate him. But that was ridiculous. Nevertheless, there was a definite look of challenge in her face.

'Katalava.' I see. Conscious that his father was enjoying his confusion, Demetri inadvertently spoke in his own language. But he quickly corrected himself. 'You are familiar with our Greek weather, Miss Manning?'

'It's Mrs Manning, actually,' she corrected him. 'But please call me Joanna, or Jo, if you prefer it.' Then, with an affectionate look at Constantine. 'Not yet. The weather, I mean. But I hope to be.'

Now, why am I not surprised?

It was all Demetri could do to prevent himself from saying the words out loud. But at least he knew a little more about her now. No one had seen fit to tell him that she'd been married. But it figured. And if he'd had any doubts about her relationship with his father they'd been dispelled by the familiarity of that look.

'Do you live on the island—um—Demetrios?' she asked suddenly, surprising him again. 'Or do you have your own home?'

'This is my home,' replied Demetri, unable to quite disguise his indignation. 'This house is our family home.' He paused. 'But do not worry, Mrs Manning. It is quite big enough to accommodate us all without any—what is it you say?—stepping on toes?'

He was pleased to see that her soft mouth tightened a little at this rebuff. The upper lip was drawn between her teeth and the lower, which was so much fuller and more vulnerable, curved protectively. Then he scowled. When had he started thinking that her mouth was soft, or vulnerable, for that matter? She was a kept woman, for heaven's sake. Hardly better than the sluts who plied their trade on the streets of Athens. He had no need to feel sorry for her. It was his father who was the vulnerable one. Vulnerable, and foolish. What on earth did he think she saw in a man at least thirty years her senior?

'Demetri has his own apartments in the house,' Constantine put in now, the look he cast at his son promising retribution later. 'As do Alex and Olivia. As my son says, this is our family home. Our island fortress, if you will. I regret you will discover that security is paramount in our situation.'

Joanna nodded. 'I understand.'

'I doubt you do,' put in Demetri pleasantly, though his feelings were anything but. 'My father is a constant target for terrorists and paparazzi alike. Only on Theapolis can we—usually—ensure that he is not at the mercy of unscrupulous men—and women.'

Her eyes flashed then, and he noticed how deep a blue they were. 'I trust you are not suggesting that I am any threat to your father?' she demanded coolly, her earlier amusement all gone now. He could hardly suppress a smile.

'Of course not,' he said, but when his dark eyes strayed to his father's taut face he saw he was by no means convinced by his son's denial. 'I am sure you and my father must have a lot in common. Tell me, Mrs Manning, do you have children, too?'

'No.'

Her answer was almost curt, but it didn't have quite the effect he'd expected. Instead of showing surprise, his father put his arm about her shoulders and drew her closer to him. Demetri was almost sure Constantine was reacting to something she'd told him, and he wondered what it was. He didn't like the idea that their relationship might be more than a temporary aberration on his father's part. A desire to prove his masculinity was one thing; a threat to his mother's memory was quite another.

But, before he could say any more, Constantine himself severed the conversation. 'Come,' he said to Joanna Manning. 'I see Nikolas Poros over there. He is a friend as well as a business colleague. I would like you to meet him.' He looked briefly at his son. 'You will excuse us?'

It was hardly a question. Although Demetri bowed his head in silent acknowledgement they both knew he wasn't being given an option. Instead, he stepped back to allow them free passage, aware as he did so that Joanna gave him a covert glance as she passed. Was it a triumphant glance? he wondered broodingly, watching them make their way across the room. He couldn't be sure. But one thing seemed apparent to him: his father's infatuation with her went deeper than the sexual fascination he had anticipated.

'Demetri! Demetri, *pos iseh*?' How are you? *'Na seh keraso kanena poto?'* Can I get you a drink?

With an effort, he became aware that there were other people around him. Neighbours; friends, relatives. They had all gathered to welcome the old man home, and his own absence until just a few minutes ago had not gone unnoticed. Forcing himself to put the problem of his father and his mistress aside, he accepted the greetings he was offered with a grim smile, aware that for the moment he was obliged to play the devoted son.

And he was devoted, dammit, he thought, taking the glass of champagne he was offered with controlled grace. But he was also his father's son, his deputy, and he couldn't help thinking that the last thing the old man needed at this time was the respect he'd always enjoyed among the shipping community weakened by some woman taking advantage of his vulnerability.

'She is beautiful, is she not?'

Spiro was at his elbow and Demetri turned to give the other man an impatient look. 'Yes, she's beautiful,' he agreed. 'But what does she want, Spiro? More importantly, what does she hope to gain from this liaison?'

'Perhaps she loves him,' suggested Spiro, accepting a glass of champagne in his turn and smiling at the dark-eyed waitress who had proffered the tray.

'And perhaps she sees him as a very convenient meal ticket,' retorted Demetri. 'My father is sixty-seven, Spiro. A woman like that does not attach herself to a much older man for love.'

'How cynical you are, Demetri.' He had been unaware that his older sister Olivia had joined them, until her soft words were whispered in his ear. 'Mrs Manning does not look like a gold-digger, you must agree.'

'How do gold-diggers look?' enquired her brother shortly, looking down into Olivia's olive-skinned face with a softening of his expression. 'Surely you are not championing her, Livvy? With only a week to go to Alex's wedding, I'd have expected you to feel as I do. After all, what is Alex going to think when she discovers our father has invited a stranger to what is essentially a family occasion?'

Olivia's lips thinned. 'Alex will not care,' she said. 'But that does not mean we can ignore the influence Mrs Manning has with Papa. And making an enemy of her may not be the wisest decision. You have seen them together. Only briefly, I admit. But you must have noticed that they seem very—absorbed with one another.'

'Absorbed, yes.' Demetri watched his father and his companion over the rim of his glass. 'How did they meet? Do we know? Where has the old man been since he got out of hospital to find a woman like her?'

Joanna's apartments adjoined Constantine's. Each suite comprised a comfortable sitting room, a spacious bedroom, and an adjoining dressing room and bathroom.

And they were sumptuously appointed. Sofas in blue and green striped linen, decorated with matching cushions, were set against walls hung with silk damask. A delicately carved writing bureau, a comprehensive entertainment centre contained in a rosewood cabinet; all were illuminated by heavy brass lamps that stood on every available surface. Long windows, closed at present, opened out onto a wraparound balcony that served all the rooms on this floor, and Turkish rugs, or kilims, splashed colour onto polished floors. There were pictures everywhere: in the sitting room, in the bedroom, even in the bathroom. And floor-length mirrors, also in the bathroom, disdained any attempt at modesty.

But it wasn't just the beauty of the things surrounding her, or their obvious value, that convinced Joanna of their exclusivity. It was the incidentals that reminded her of where she was and why she was there. The sheets being changed every day, for example; the expensive cosmetics and toiletries removed and replaced as soon as she used them; the knowledge that she had only to touch the bell for her smallest wish to be granted.

This was Constantine's world, she thought ruefully. The way he lived. She had never known such assiduous attention to detail, and although she had agreed to come here for Constantine's sake, she had never imagined anything like this.

She couldn't help wishing he had not been so *rich*.

Not that his son would believe that, she thought drily, wondering if Constantine had glimpsed the momentary flash of hatred in Demetrios's dark eyes. He probably had. Constantine must know exactly how his son was feeling. After all, that was why he had persuaded her to come here. He'd known that nothing short of grim hostility would blind Demetrios to the truth.

There was a light tap on the panelled double doors that connected her apartments to Constantine's. Joanna, who had been trying to decide what she should wear for dinner that evening, hurried to answer it. She'd guessed that it was Constantine, and it was. But, just in case, she'd wanted to make sure before inviting anyone else into her room.

'May I come in?'

'Of course.' Joanna stood back to allow him into her sitting room, gazing at him intently. He'd shed his formal clothes, as she had, and he looked so frail now that the necessity to appear invincible was gone. She indicated one of the overstuffed sofas. 'Sit down. You're supposed to be resting, you know.'

'You are not my nurse, Joanna.' Constantine's smile was warm but defensive. He was wearing a white towelling bathrobe and the colour accentuated his pallor. 'As a matter of fact, I am feeling a little stronger this evening. Now that Demetri is home I can relax.'

'Oh, right.' Joanna closed the door behind him, tucking the folds of the scarlet wrapper she'd put on after her shower closer about her. 'I suppose that's because you think the worst is over.' She shook her head. 'I wouldn't hold my breath, if I were you.'

'Joanna, Joanna.' Constantine sighed, but he took her advice and subsided onto the nearest sofa. 'Do not be so cynical, my dear. Just because Demetri is not entirely happy with the situation— and, I admit, I believe he does have doubts about the suitability of our relationship—he will do nothing to jeopardise the peace of the household. Not with Alex's wedding to consider. I am his father, Joanna. I think I know him better than anyone else.'

'Do you?'

Joanna wished she could feel as sure. Her own encounter with Demetrios Kastro had left a decidedly unpleasant taste in her mouth. She was convinced that he had nothing but contempt for her, that he believed she was only with his father for what she hoped to get out of him. He had been polite, but cold; saying little, but implying a lot.

She was glad he hadn't deceived his father, but she was afraid Constantine was deluding himself if he thought Demetrios had accepted her presence.

'Anyway,' Constantine said now, reaching out to take her hand and urge her down beside him, 'how are you? Are you happy here? Do you have everything you need?'

'Need you ask?' Joanna was rueful. 'This place is amazing. It's everything you said it was and more.'

'I am glad.' Constantine raised her hand to his dry lips. 'I want you to enjoy your stay. I want you to feel at home here. I know Demetri may be difficult for a while, but he will get over it. Besides, so long as I am ostensibly recuperating he will have little time to fret about our relationship. Between now and the wedding there may be occasions when he has to leave the island. With my work to do as well as his own...' He allowed the words to trail away. 'You understand?'

'I can't wait.' Joanna pulled a wry face. Then, withdrawing her hand from his, she got to her feet again. 'But are you sure about this? What is Alex going to think when she finds out I'm here?'

'Alex will love you,' said Constantine firmly. 'She is not like Demetri or Olivia. She is younger; less cynical, shall we say?'

'All the same…' Joanna lifted the heavy weight of her loosened hair from her neck, enjoying the coolness of the air-conditioning on her hot skin. 'I can still go back to England, Constantine. I wouldn't mind.'

'I would.' His response was unequivocal. 'My dear, the reasons I asked you to come to Theapolis have not changed. I need you. I need your strength and your companionship. And, most of all, I need your support.'

'You have that, of course.' Joanna sighed. 'I'm just not sure whether I can go through with it.'

Constantine pushed himself to his feet. 'Because of me?' he asked. 'You find me so repulsive?'

'Don't be silly.' Joanna touched his cheek with a tender hand. 'You're a very attractive man. I've always thought so.'

'You have?' He was sceptical.

'Yes.' She hesitated a moment, and then cupped his face between her palms and bestowed a warm kiss at the corner of his mouth. 'Now, stop fishing for compliments and tell me what you think I should wear for dinner this evening.'

'What you are wearing at present seems eminently suitable to me,' declared Constantine gallantly, his hands reaching for her waist to hold her in front of him. 'You always look beautiful.'

Joanna shook her head, but before she could think of a response there was a knock at the outer door.

'Beno mesa!'

Almost automatically Constantine replied, bidding the caller to enter, and Joanna turned her head as the foyer door opened.

Demetrios appeared moments later, pausing on the threshold of the sitting room. He, too, had evidently taken a shower. Water sparkled on the sleek darkness of his hair, contrasting with the pearl-grey elegance of his suit. A dark blue, body-hugging tee shirt completed his outfit, and Joanna was instantly conscious of the intimacy of the scene he had interrupted. Both she and Constantine were scantily clad, and Constantine's hands on her body looked undeniably possessive.

She didn't know which of them was the most disconcerted by Demetrios's arrival. To his credit, Constantine seemed only mildly curious about his son's purpose in coming here, but Joanna was definitely uneasy. And Demetrios himself was evidently taken aback by his father's presence in her suite.

Yet, what had he expected? she asked herself a little wildly. Why did he think Constantine had brought her here, if not to enjoy her company? Surely he didn't think his father was too old to

enjoy female companionship? And, most perti-
nently of all, what was he doing coming to her
apartments uninvited? If anyone had any explain-
ing to do, it was him.

CHAPTER TWO

'DEMETRI?'

His father was obviously waiting for an explanation, but right now Demetri didn't have one to give him. He was still stunned by the sight of his father's hands on Joanna Manning's hips. Brown hands, already showing the spots of age, were dark against the scarlet satin of her wrapper. A wrapper that he suspected was all she was wearing. *Khristo*, what had they been doing? Taking a shower together?

His imagination ran riot. He hadn't realised her hair would be so long, but she had evidently washed it and now it tumbled pale and silky about her shoulders. The scarlet wrapper, too, was unknowingly provocative, drawing his attention to the slender shapeliness of her body, outlining her hips and the long, long length of her legs.

To his disgust, his body stirred. He could feel his arousal pushing against the hand he'd thrust into his trouser pocket, and he quickly withdrew it. Then, angry at the immaturity of his reaction, he tried to pull himself together. His father was waiting for a reply and he had no wish for the old man to guess he was in any way attracted to his—he sought for a suitably insulting description—his paramour.

'I—good evening, Papa, Mrs Manning,' he essayed politely. 'I trust you have found everything to your satisfaction?'

His father's brows drew together. 'We have been here two days already, Demetri,' he reminded his son shortly. His hands fell away from Joanna's body. 'I cannot believe that concern for our welfare is the reason you have chosen to invade our privacy at this time.'

It wasn't, of course. But then, he hadn't expected to encounter his father at all. It was Mrs Manning he had come to see. He had hoped—rather foolishly, he acknowledged now—that they might have a few moments of private conversation before his father interrupted them.

'I—wanted to speak to you, Papa,' he said, improvising swiftly. And perhaps it was just as well that his father was here after all, he conceded. His reaction to this woman had been totally unexpected, and it would have been horribly embarrassing if Constantine had not been there and she had noticed his discomfort. *Theos!* The back of his neck was sweating. What the hell was the matter with him?

'And you surmised I would be here, with Joanna?'

His father was not a fool, and Demetri had to think fast to find an answer. 'I—tried your apartments, but could get no reply,' he muttered, hoping that Philip, his father's manservant, wouldn't contradict him. 'But it doesn't matter now. I can see you are—' the words almost stuck in his throat '—occupied with other things. It can wait until tomorrow.'

'I am sure it can.' Constantine was clearly waiting for him to leave, and Demetri permitted himself only a brief glance at Joanna before striding out of the room.

In the hall outside, Demetri paused for a moment, breathing deeply and running decidedly unsteady hands through the thickness of his hair. He felt unnerved, shaken, and although he knew he should get the hell away from there, he was strangely reluctant to do so. It felt as if the image of the two of them together was emblazoned on his memory, and he knew it was going to take more than the slamming of a door to get it out of his head. And how sensible was that?

He glanced back over his shoulder, half-afraid that he was being observed, but the door was still firmly closed and no sounds were audible from within. His father and his mistress had evidently

resumed whatever it was they had been doing before his arrival, and he didn't need a crystal ball
to guess what that was.

Na pari i oryi!

He swore silently, and then, gathering himself,
strode back along the corridor to the galleried
landing at the head of the stairs. He was going to
have a great influence on his father's behaviour
if he started lusting after Mrs Manning himself,
he thought contemptuously. When had he begun
thinking with his sex instead of with his head?

The salon had been cleared in his absence. The
huge reception room, which had earlier been
thronged with the guests his sister had invited to
welcome his father home, was now restored to its
usual appearance. The furniture, which had
mostly been moved aside during the reception,
had now been gathered into small groupings, with
tall crystal vases and porcelain urns spilling
glossy blossoms onto every available surface. The
scent of the flowers was pungent, dispelling the
smells of tobacco and stale perfume. Someone
had turned up the air-conditioning so that the
room was decidedly chilly, but he wished it was
earlier in the year so that he could fold back the
long glass doors that opened onto the floodlit terrace. It would have been nice to allow the soft
evening air to cool his overheated senses, but that

wasn't an option. At this time of the year there were too many insects flying about, and he didn't wish to be bitten half to death.

'Can I get you anything, sir?'

Demetri swung round to find a member of the household staff hovering behind him. He was tempted to order a bottle of Scotch and take himself off to the farthest corner of the estate and get thoroughly and disgustingly drunk. But he was not his father's son for nothing, and Kastros did not make fools of themselves, particularly not in front of the servants.

'Nothing, thanks,' he responded now, waving the man away. Then he flung himself down into a cream velvet armchair and stared broodingly out of the windows.

Spiro found him there perhaps ten minutes later. The lamplit room was shadowy, and Demetri had chosen to sit in the darkest corner, but Spiro's eyes were sharp. Like his employer, he, too, had changed for the evening, wearing a shirt and tie instead of the casual polo shirts he preferred.

'I believe your sister and the other guests who are staying for dinner have gathered in the library,' he said, advancing across the room. 'What are you doing in here? Sulking?'

'Watch your tongue,' said Demetri shortly, and Spiro arched a wounded brow.

'I gather you were sent away with your tail between your legs,' he observed, ignoring the reproof. 'What is the matter? Did she tell you she was playing for bigger stakes?'

'Do not be stupid!' Demetri placed his hands on the arms of the chair and pushed himself to his feet. He glanced around. 'Is there anything to drink in here?'

Spiro pushed his hands into his trouser pockets and swayed back on his heels, surveying the large room with a considering eye. 'It does not look like it,' he said. 'Why do we not join your father's guests? There is a bar in the library.'

'Thank you, I know that,' retorted Demetri, scowling. 'Look, why do you not go and join the party? I am—not in the mood for company.'

'Why not?'

'*Theos*, Spiro, mind your own damn business!' Demetri heaved a frustrated breath. 'You are not my keeper, you know.'

Spiro shrugged his shoulders. 'So you did lose out?'

'No!' Demetri stared at his friend with angry eyes. Then, when Spiro didn't back down, he gave a resigned shake of his head. 'All right. I

did not even get to speak to her. No pain, no gain.
Does that answer your question?'

'Not really.' Spiro waited. 'Was she not in her
own apartments?'

'Oh, yes.' Demetri was sardonic. 'She was
there. She just was not alone, that is all.'

Spiro's mouth formed a pronounced circle.
'Oh,' he said drily. 'Well, there is always tomorrow.'

'Yeah.' Demetri was ironic. 'And tomorrow
and tomorrow,' he acceded flatly. 'Come. Let us
go and find a drink. I do not want the old man to
think I have got anything to hide.'

'Do you think he has?'

'Who knows?' Demetri made a careless gesture. 'I wonder why he has brought her here.'

Spiro pulled a face. 'I think I can hazard a
guess,' he remarked, and Demetri gave him an
impatient look.

'Yeah, right,' he said shortly. 'She is to be his
guest at Alex's wedding.' He frowned. 'I wonder
where Mr Manning is.'

'If there is a Mr Manning.'

'You think she is lying?'

'No.' Spiro shook his head. 'But she is not
wearing a ring. Do you think she is divorced?'

'Who knows?' Demetri was weary of the
whole conversation. 'Rings do not mean a lot

these days. Besides, what does it signify? She is here. That is the only thing that matters.'

'Do you think their relationship is serious?'

Demetri was taken aback. 'Do you?'

'Perhaps.' Spiro looked pensive. 'Your father seems to care about her. Do you not think so?'

Demetri scowled. 'So what are you saying? That he intends to marry her?'

'Hardly that.' Spiro drew in a breath as they started towards the door. 'But serious illness can do strange things to people, *filos mou*. Being reminded of your own mortality can leave you with a desperate desire to embrace life.'

Demetri snorted. 'Since when did you become a philosopher?'

'I am just trying to be objective,' Spiro protested. 'And, despite reports to the contrary, Mrs Manning does not give me the impression that her relationship with your father is purely for financial gain.'

'You feel you know her that well?' Demetri was scornful.

'No.' Spiro was defensive now. 'But I have been here since yesterday, when they arrived. I have watched them together. And, if I was scrupulously honest, I would say that they have known one another a considerable length of time.'

* * *

'Have you known my father long?'

The question was asked by a slim dark woman, whose resemblance to her father was unmistakable. Constantine had told Joanna that Olivia, too, had married when she was nineteen. But the marriage hadn't lasted. In Constantine's opinion Olivia had been too spoilt, too headstrong, to submit to her ex-husband's needs. Within months of wedding Andrea Petrou she had returned to Theapolis, and since then she had shown no serious interest in any other man.

Joanna knew that Olivia was the eldest of Constantine's three children. At thirty-six, she considered herself the mistress of his house, which was perhaps why she was viewing Joanna with such suspicion. Maybe she saw the other woman as a challenge to her authority, and Joanna was glad that her ankle-length beaded sheath bore favourable comparison with the froth of chiffon that Olivia was wearing.

She had cornered Joanna beside the polished cabinets that housed her father's collection of snuffboxes. She had chosen her moment, and Joanna realised she had been a little foolish to walk away from Constantine and lay herself open to cross-examination.

'Quite long,' she responded now, directing her attention to the jewelled items that had drawn her across the room in the first place. She had delivered many of these boxes to Constantine herself, and it was fascinating to see them all together in the display case. Aware that Olivia was still beside her, she added, 'Aren't these beautiful?'

'Valuable, certainly,' said Olivia insolently. 'Are you interested in antiques, Mrs Manning?'

Joanna ignored the implication and, taking the woman's words at face value, she replied, 'I—I work with antiques, actually.' She paused. 'As a matter of fact, that is how I met your father.'

Olivia's thin brows elevated. 'Really?'

'Yes, really.' Joanna chose her words with care. 'I work for an auction house.'

'An auction house?' Olivia immediately picked up on the information. 'In London?'

'That's right.' Joanna allowed a little sigh to escape her. 'What do you do, Mrs Petrou?'

'What do I do?'

Olivia was clearly taken aback, but before she could say anything more her father came to join them. Slipping an arm about Joanna's waist, he said, 'Well, let me see: she is a fabulous dancer, an expert at water sports, and extremely good at spending money. My money,' he added drily. 'Is that not so, Livvy? Have I missed anything out?'

'Because you will not let me do anything else,' retorted Olivia shortly. Then, struggling to contain her anger, 'In any case, I do not think it is any of Mrs Manning's business.'

Joanna was unhappily aware that she had made another enemy. It was obvious that none of Constantine's offspring would blame *him* for his indiscretions. As far as they were concerned, she had instigated this whole affair.

Deciding there was nothing she could say which would placate Olivia, she turned to Constantine instead. 'How are you?' she asked, before he could remonstrate with his daughter. 'You're looking tired. Are you sure you wouldn't rather eat upstairs?'

'I am sure *you* would,' murmured Constantine, for her ears only. But, for all his attempt at humour, he was looking drained. The day had taken a toll on his depleted resources and he should have been resting. But she had always admired his strength of spirit, and he demonstrated it again now. 'How could I desert our guests? Besides, I am ready for my dinner,' he averred, his smile warm and enveloping. 'Are you?'

Knowing better than to argue with him, Joanna tucked her arm through his. 'Is it time to go in?'

'When I have finished this,' agreed Constantine, indicating the remnants of the spirit in his glass. He held the glass up to a nearby lamp. 'Do you know, you can only get real ouzo in Greece? I have tried it elsewhere, but it is never the same.'

'Ought you to be drinking alcohol, Papa?' Olivia had been observing their exchange in silence, but now she took his other arm. 'You have been ill, Papa. I worry about you.' She glanced disparagingly at Joanna. 'It is important that you do not overstretch your strength.'

Constantine's lips tightened. 'I am delighted that you are so concerned for my welfare, Livvy. But I am sure Demetri has told you I am very well. Besides, I have the beautiful Joanna to look after me. I have to tell you, she can be as strict as the most costly physician.'

And twice as expensive. Joanna could practically hear what Olivia was thinking, but she held her tongue. And then Demetrios entered the room, and his sister's eyes turned in his direction. Joanna grimaced. Was she conceivably going to be grateful to Constantine's son for diverting Olivia's attention from herself?

Spiro Stavros was with his employer. Both men were in their early thirties, but Spiro possessed none of Demetrios's brooding good looks. Nevertheless, they were both tall and powerfully built. But Joanna decided she preferred Spiro's open countenance to Demetrios's cold eyes and dark beauty.

Olivia left her father's side to greet her brother, and Constantine took the opportunity to speak privately to Joanna. 'Do not let anything Livvy or Demetri say upset you,' he murmured softly. 'They are curious, that is all. So long as you play your part, and do not allow anyone to coerce you into some unguarded admission, all will be well.'

Joanna wished she could feel as confident. She wasn't used to any of this, not to Constantine's wealth, or his influence, or the feeling that every other person she met thought she was a fortune-hunter. She wasn't. She wasn't interested in Constantine's money. But she'd also realised that the doubts she'd had in England had been justified. Indeed, they were rapidly developing into a full-blown belief that she shouldn't be here.

'Do you think they believe we're lovers?' she asked in a low voice, and Constantine grinned with a little of his old arrogance.

'Oh, yes. They believe it,' he said, permitting himself a brief glance in his son's direction. 'And do you know what?' He arched a teasing brow. 'I am beginning to enjoy it.'

Dinner was served in what Constantine told her was the family dining salon, but it seemed awfully big to Joanna. She was sure her whole apartment back in London would have fitted into this one room, and she thought it was just as well that the Greek islands didn't suffer the extremes of temperature that England did. Heating this place would be a nightmare, she reflected, glancing round the high-ceilinged room with its imposing furniture and marble floor.

Last evening she and Constantine had dined in his suite, and that hadn't been half so intimidating. Although it had been her first evening, and the assiduous attention of the servants had been a little unnerving, she had enjoyed the meal. She had still been entranced by the beauty of her surroundings, and she'd managed to persuade herself that this wasn't going to be as bad as she'd thought.

How wrong she'd been!

Nevertheless, Olivia's claws had been sheathed at that first meeting. With Alex away at her fiancé's home in Athens, and Demetri meeting with bankers in Geneva, Olivia had been alone and unprepared for Joanna's arrival. Joanna had wondered if Constantine had really warned his family of his guest's identity. He'd insisted he had, but there'd been no doubt that Olivia had been shocked by their relationship.

Joanna sighed. She had spent most of the day avoiding the other woman's questions and now she had Demetrios to contend with as well. She wondered if Constantine had realised how hostile his family would be. Despite his reassurances about Alex, she thought that was little consolation now.

The food, as she'd already discovered, was exquisitely prepared. There were *dolmades*—lamb and spiced rice wrapped in vine leaves, and *souvlakia*—which were tiny chunks of pork grilled on skewers. There were tomatoes stuffed with goat's cheese, cold meats and salads, and retsina, the clean aromatic wine of the region, which was flavoured with pine resin and was, to Joanna, an acquired taste.

As well as Constantine's son and daughter, and Spiro Stavros, of course, they were joined at the table by three other people. They were Nikolas Poros and his wife, who Constantine had introduced her to earlier, and an old uncle of Constantine's second wife, who also lived at the villa. Panos Petronides was in his eighties, but he seemed years younger. He was still as alert and spry as he'd been when he'd first left his native Salonika.

Conversation during the meal was, to Joanna's relief, sporadic. She suspected that for all his assertions to the contrary Constantine was tired, and she found herself watching him anxiously, ready for any sign that he needed to escape. Demetrios had been more right than he knew when he'd questioned his father's return to the island. Constantine was very weak, and Joanna hoped he could keep up the pretence until the wedding was over.

Coffee, strong and black, was served in the adjoining drawing room. Joanna had hoped that Constantine might make their excuses and allow them both to escape to their own apartments. But, instead, he settled himself on a silk-cushioned sofa, drawing her down beside him to prevent Olivia from taking her place.

He indicated the silver dishes of sticky sugar-coated pastries on the low table close by. 'Please,' he said. 'Help yourself.'

Joanna, who had eaten little of her dinner, shook her head. 'I don't want anything else,' she said, aware of Demetrios hovering close by, ostensibly studying the rich desserts. She waited until he had chosen a cheese-filled pastry dusted with cinnamon sugar and then retired to the nearest armchair before she felt able to continue. 'May I get you something instead?'

'Not to eat,' murmured Constantine archly, provoking a scowling look from his son. Then, to Demetrios, 'We will talk in the morning. You can brief me on all that has happened since I have been away. For instance, I understand from Nikolas Poros that two of our tankers are lying idle at Piraeus. I hope you have an explanation for that.'

'They are not lying idle,' retorted Demetrios, hot colour filling his angry face. 'Did not Poros explain that—?'

'Tomorrow, Demetri,' said his father finally. Then, to Joanna's relief, he turned to her. 'I am a little tired, *agapi mou*. Are you finished?'

'I—yes, of course.'

'But surely you are not going to deprive us of Mrs Manning's company also?' Demetrios broke in, earning his father's displeasure yet again. Joanna felt Constantine stiffen beside her.

'You have something else in mind, *agori*?' he asked, and Demetrios offered a courteous smile.

'I wondered if Mrs Manning might enjoy a stroll in the gardens,' he suggested mildly, but Joanna detected the look that passed between him and Spiro Stavros as he spoke. 'I believe the English are very fond of gardening. Am I not right, Mrs Manning?'

'I'm afraid I live in a high-rise, Mr Kastro,' Joanna returned carefully, but Constantine intervened before she could say anything more.

'Joanna is tired, too,' he declared, but Demetrios was determined to have the last word.

'Are you sure, Papa? Dare I say it? She is—considerably younger than you are.'

'You overstep yourself, Demetri.' There was no mistaking Constantine's anger now, and Joanna wished she could warn the younger man to back off.

'Perhaps you should let Mrs Manning decide for herself,' he persisted smoothly, and Joanna heaved a heavy sigh.

'I fear your father is right,' she told him coolly, aware that he probably thought she was taking the easy way out. 'I am tired. It has been a—demanding day.'

Demetrios's lips twisted. 'I am sure it must have been,' he remarked, and although his words were polite enough his meaning was plain. He got abruptly to his feet. 'Then, if you will excuse me...' And without waiting for his father's permission he stalked out of the room.

CHAPTER THREE

DESPITE the heat in the early-morning air, the pool was cold. Later in the day, when the sun had done its work, the temperature of the water would rise. But right now it was decidedly chilly, and Demetri welcomed its cooling surge against his hot skin.

He had not slept well. Indeed, he had slept exceedingly badly, tormented by dreams the nature of which he preferred not to dwell on now that he was awake. In fact, he was frustrated by his own inability to control his subconscious mind, and only several vigorous lengths of the pool offered some escape from his tortured senses.

He swam swiftly from one end of the pool to the other, somersaulting beneath the surface to swim back underwater. He broke through the waves his body had created, desperate for air, and then saw that he was no longer alone.

A woman had emerged from the villa. She hadn't seen him. It was obvious from the unhurried way she crossed the sun-splashed patio to rest her hands on the terrace wall. Obvious, too, from the uninhibited way she tilted back her head and allowed the sun to kiss those pale exquisite features.

She thought she was alone, and Demetri felt a momentary pang of shame in observing her this way. But dammit, he thought, he had more right to be here than she had, and it wasn't his fault if she didn't have the sense to ensure she was on her own before behaving like a pagan goddess, worshipping the dawn.

She was beautiful, though. Given this opportunity to study her without her knowledge, Demetri had to admit he understood his father's fascination. She was wearing a sleeveless vest this morning, something soft and silky that clung to her rounded breasts with a loving attention to detail. He caught his breath as she cupped her ribcage and arched her back, driving her taut nipples against the thin fabric. A loosely tied sarong circled her waist, a transparent thing of purples and greens that exposed the bikini briefs she wore beneath. It parted to reveal the slender length of her legs, and, despite the coolness of the water, Demetri felt himself harden.

Theos! He was like a callow youth, he thought exasperatedly. She was beautiful, yes, but he'd seen beautiful women before. He hadn't reached the mature age of thirty-four without making love to a number of them, too, and it irritated the hell out of him that he desired *this* woman, his father's mistress.

She was sliding her fingers into her hair now, scooping its loosened weight back from her face and winding it into a coil on top of her head. Soft tendrils tumbled from the impromptu knot, spiralling down against cheeks that were as smooth and velvety soft as a peach. Realising he couldn't stand much more of this without disgracing himself completely, Demetri sprang out of the water and grabbed a towel to wrap protectively about his hips.

She heard him, of course. Although the ocean surged constantly onto the beach only a couple of hundred yards from the villa it was a muted sound, heavy and rhythmic. His vaulting out of the pool was a much more abrasive sound, and she swung round almost guiltily to confront him.

'Oh…' She was clearly taken aback by his sudden appearance. 'Um—Mr Kastro. I didn't see you there.'

'No.' Demetri acknowledged the fact, and, accepting that they couldn't go on addressing each other across the width of the terrace, he pushed his damp feet into his deck shoes and walked towards her. 'Did you sleep well?'

She managed a faint smile. 'Like you care,' she said drily, and he admired her courage. 'Did you?'

Demetri shrugged his bare shoulders. 'Not very,' he conceded, just as candidly. Then, dragging his eyes back to her face, 'Where is my father?'

'Where do you think he is at this hour of the morning?' she asked, a delicate flush invading her cheeks. 'He's still in bed.' She paused a moment and then added significantly, 'Asleep.'

Demetri's mouth compressed. 'So, what are you doing up so early? Or is this your only chance to escape?'

'To escape?' Her blue eyes flashed with anger. 'To escape from what, Mr Kastro? Your father and I have a perfect understanding.'

'Do you?' Demetri was annoyed to find he half believed her. But he couldn't let her know it. 'That must be very convenient for both of you.'

'It is.' She turned away from him then, bracing her hands on the terrace wall again and gazing purposefully out to sea. 'Oughtn't you to go and get some clothes on, Mr Kastro? I shouldn't like you to catch a chill.'

'Oh, I am sure you would,' he corrected her, making no move to go back into the villa. 'But I would hate to waste this opportunity for us to get to know one another better.'

'We don't need to get to know one another better, Mr Kastro,' she retorted, and although she wasn't looking at him he could see the tension in the slender cords of her neck.

'Well, there, you see, you are wrong,' he argued softly, resisting the temptation to run his finger along the sensitive curve of her nape. He drew a steadying breath. 'And I think we can dispense with formality, no?'

She licked her lips then, and his stomach twisted with sudden emotion. *Theos*, he thought, the intensity of his reaction reminding him that he was playing with fire here. Why was he persisting with this? It was his father he should be harassing, not her.

'What formality are you talking about?' she asked now, and he had to concentrate hard to remember what he'd said.

'I—think you should call me Demetri,' he essayed at last, congratulating himself on his memory. 'May I call you Joanna?'

Her lips were pressed together when she turned to give him a doubtful look, and Demetri guessed she had expected some kind of accusation. Long lashes, several shades darker than her hair, shaded her expression, however, and instead of feeling any sense of triumph Demetri found himself imagining how they would feel against his lips. He wanted to kiss her, he realised suddenly. He wanted to press that slim luscious body against his own and ease his aching need between her legs…

'I don't think that's a very good idea, Mr Kastro,' she said, and his arousal abruptly deflated. 'You don't like me, so why pretend you want to get to know me?'

Why indeed?

'Because I do,' he insisted, deciding that he had nothing more to lose. 'Why are you so afraid to talk to me?' His dark brows elevated. 'I am not so terrifying, am I?'

She turned then, resting her hips on the low wall behind her and folding her arms across her midriff. 'I am not afraid to talk to you, Mr Kastro,' she said, and once again he had to admire her spirit. 'What do you want to talk about?'

Demetri's hair was dripping onto his neck and he lifted one hand to wipe the moisture from his nape. He refused to accept that it was done to buy himself a little time, but there was no doubt that she had caught him off guard.

'*Entaxi.*' It was an indication of his state of mind that had him lapsing into his own language for the exclamation. 'All right. Tell me how you met my father?'

There was a perceptible hesitation when that tempting tongue appeared again, and then she seemed to straighten her spine before saying slowly, 'We met in London.'

Demetri gave her a dry look. 'Yes. I had gathered that.' He paused. 'I asked how you met my father, Mrs Manning. Not where.'

She looked down at her feet then, and Demetri found himself doing the same, watching as she crossed one slim bare foot over the other. Until then he hadn't realised she wasn't wearing any shoes, and there was something infinitely sensuous about the way she rubbed the sole of one foot across the arch of the other.

To distract himself, he spoke again, his words a little harsh as he struggled to sustain his composure. 'Were you his nurse?'

'His nurse?' She smiled then, and he was treated to the sight of a row of almost perfect white teeth. 'Heavens, no!'

'What, then?' Demetri was impatient at the way she could apparently best him at every turn. 'His doctor?'

She shook her head, and her hair dipped confidingly over one shoulder. 'I am not a member of the medical profession, Mr Kastro.'

Demetri's nostrils flared. 'Do not play with me, Mrs Manning. You might just get more than you—what is the expression you use?—bargained for, no?'

Her smile disappeared. 'I wouldn't dream of playing with you, Mr Kastro,' she declared coolly. 'I just wonder why you are so interested in what I do for a living.'

'I am not.' But he was and she knew it, damn her. 'I am merely curious to know how a man who has spent the last two weeks in hospital could have acquired such a—close relationship with a woman his family knew nothing about.'

She took a deep breath. 'As you say, your father has been in hospital.'

'Where I visited him,' put in Demetri shortly. 'On more than one occasion. Yet he apparently chose not to mention your existence to me.'

Her slim shoulders lifted. 'I suppose he preferred to wait until we could be introduced.'

'You are prevaricating again, Mrs Manning.' Demetri's temper was slipping. 'I suggest that, far from knowing my father for some considerable time, as you told Livvy, yours has been what a kinder person might call a whirlwind romance, no?'

'No.' She was angry now. 'What I told your sister was—*is* true. I work—I have worked—for Bartholomew's for several years. They're—'

'One of the foremost auction houses in London,' Demetri inserted tersely. 'I have heard of Bartholomew's, Mrs Manning.'

'Good.' Her eyes challenged his. 'As you're aware, your father is a keen collector of antique snuffboxes. He has been a regular customer there for many years.'

Demetri was stunned. He was ashamed to admit that, because of her beauty, he'd been inclined to dismiss her as an airhead. Now, learning that she had a career far removed from any cosmetic pursuit disturbed him more than he cared to admit. It also made her relationship with his father that much more serious somehow.

'And now, if you'll excuse me…'

She was leaving him, and Demetri could no longer think of an excuse to keep her there. But what troubled him most was that he should want to do so, and he abruptly stepped aside, opening her path to the villa.

'Until later,' he said, but she didn't answer him. If he hadn't known better he'd have said she was trembling with apprehension. Only it wasn't apprehension, it was rage.

*　　*　　*

Joanna made it to her apartments before she gave in to the fit of shaking that had threatened her downstairs. Dear Lord, she thought, she would never have ventured outdoors if she'd even suspected she might run into Demetrios Kastro on the patio. A naked Demetrios Kastro, moreover. Her mouth dried again at the thought.

But she'd looked over her balcony and there'd appeared to be no one about. Oh, she'd seen a couple of men working in the gardens, and a youth of perhaps fifteen sweeping the steps. Yet even he had disappeared by the time she'd stepped out of the villa, and she'd walked to the boundary wall with the first feeling of freedom she'd had since coming here.

And the view was so beautiful. Acres of flower-filled gardens falling away into dunes of sun-bleached sand. A wooden jetty pointed into the blue-green waters of the Aegean, a two-masted schooner bobbing at anchor, all gleaming steel and polished teak. A millionaire's plaything in a million-dollar setting.

Then Demetrios had emerged from the pool and everything had changed. Her sense of well-being had vanished, replaced by the tension that man always evoked. She'd known him for less than twenty-four hours, yet he'd already succeeded in setting her nerves on edge whenever he was near. She had the feeling he looked at her and saw right through her. He didn't like her: that much was obvious. But, more than that, he despised her for what he thought she was doing with his father.

Now Joanna wrapped her arms about herself and crossed the room to the windows. Despite her revulsion for the man, she felt compelled to see if he was still enjoying his swim. She had only interrupted his pleasure. He had destroyed hers.

But the pool was empty. Although she waited half apprehensively to see if he was briefly out of sight, hidden by the lip of the deck, he didn't appear. The water was as smooth and unbroken as a mirror, reflecting only the sunlight and the waving palms that grew close by.

Stepping back into the room again, she looked bleakly about her. And then, annoyed that she had let Demetrios sour her mood, she walked through the bedroom and into the adjoining bathroom.

She felt a little better after a shower. The cool water had washed away the perspiration that had dried on her skin, and she felt more ready to face the day. Constantine had said he would take her to the small town of Agios Antonis this morning, and she was looking forward to seeing a little more of the island. Since their arrival two days ago they had spent all their time at the villa.

Constantine had been weary after the flight from London, and yesterday he had had the reception Olivia had organised to contend with. Joanna knew he would have much preferred to stagger the celebrations for his homecoming, but Constantine hadn't wanted to disappoint his elder daughter. Besides, until his younger daughter's wedding was over he didn't intend to discuss his illness with any of his family.

Joanna finished drying her hair and paused on the threshold of the dressing room that was next to the bathroom. Floor-to-ceiling closets lined two of the walls, but the clothes she had brought with her looked lost in their cavernous depths.

Nevertheless, Constantine had insisted on equipping her with several new outfits for the trip to Theapolis. And, although Joanna still felt slightly uncomfortable about that arrangement, she had to admit that the clothes she usually favoured would not have borne comparison with the designer fashions she had seen since their arrival.

The fact that she normally shunned anything that emphasised her femininity had not been lost on Constantine. And, despite the fact that he respected her preference for severe skirt- and trouser-suits, he had persuaded her that they would definitely look out of place in the hot dry climate of the island in late summer.

Besides, they would have detracted from the image he wanted her to present. It was because she could do what he asked that he'd chosen her, and in the circumstances Joanna had been unable to refuse.

Perhaps she'd wanted to do it for her own sake, she reflected, riffling through the rail of expensive garments, all of which were designed to inspire and provoke masculine attention. Flimsy shirts and tight-fitting basques; low-cut bodices and clinging skirts; hems slashed to expose her legs from thigh to hip—items that until two weeks ago she'd have avoided like the plague.

But it hadn't always been so. Once she would have revelled in their style and beauty. Oh, she had never owned anything too revealing, but she had appreciated her own body and dressed in a way to make the most of her assets. She'd spent so many years believing she was worthless that when the opportunity had come to make the most of her appearance, she'd taken it. She'd wanted to be admired. She'd wanted to know the thrill of feeling beautiful.

And then she'd met Richard Manning...

But she didn't want to think about Richard now. He was history. He'd hurt and humiliated her for the last time. But perhaps by downplaying her looks she'd been subconsciously denying their relationship. Maybe it was time to come out of her shell.

She viewed her appearance cautiously when she was ready. It would take some time before she was able to look at herself with uncritical eyes, and although the lime-green crêpe shell and cream silk shorts were very flattering, she couldn't get used to exposing such a length of thigh. Still, she was sure Constantine would approve and, for the present, that was all that mattered.

Which reminded her—where was Constantine? He had said he would order breakfast to be served on the balcony again, as he had done the previous morning, but when she stepped outside again there was still no one about. The wrought-iron table wasn't even laid, and she knew a moment's apprehension. What was going on? Surely Demetrios hadn't delayed him. His son had been eager to speak to him, it was true, but all the same…

Turning back into the room, she crossed to the connecting doors and tapped lightly on the panels. It was the first time she had had to initiate their meeting, and she felt a little awkward when Philip, Constantine's valet, opened the door.

'*Kalimera*, Kiria Manning.' The man greeted her politely enough, though she sensed a certain reserve in his manner. '*Boro na sas voithisso?*'

Joanna contained her impatience. Constantine had told his valet that she didn't understand his language, and therefore the man's behaviour was a deliberate attempt to disconcert her.

However, she had taken the precaution of learning one phrase, and with smiling courtesy she said, '*Then katalaveno,*' which she knew meant, I don't understand. '*Signomi.*' Sorry.

Philip's thin lips tightened. He was a man in his late fifties, who Constantine had said had been with him for more than thirty years. Gaunt and unsmiling, he was the exact opposite of Joanna's idea of a genial manservant, his only concession to vanity the luxuriant black moustache that coated his upper lip.

'Kirie Kastro is not—up, *kiria*,' he said at last, in a thick barely comprehensible accent. '*Then sikothikeh akomi.*'

Joanna frowned, looking beyond him into the living area of Constantine's suite. The door to the bedroom was ajar, but she couldn't see into the room, and she could only take Philip's word that Constantine was still in bed.

'Is he all right?' she asked, not much caring if the valet cared to stand here trading information with her. 'Can I see him?'

'I do not think—'

'*Pios ineh*, Philip?' Who is it?

Constantine's voice was frail, but he had obviously deduced that the manservant was talking to someone, and, ignoring Philip's attempt to bar her way, Joanna sidestepped him into the apartment. 'It's me, Constantine,' she called, crossing the floor to the bedroom door. 'Can I come in?'

'Please…'

Constantine showed no reservations about inviting her into his room. And why should he? she asked herself drily. When they were deemed to be lovers.

All the same, she halted in the doorway of the huge, distinctly masculine chamber, briefly shocked by his appearance. Constantine was lying propped against the pillows of the massive bed, his face as white as the linen sheets that covered him from chest to foot. Brown hands, slightly gnarled with veins, were a stark contrast to the bedlinen, his nails scraping against the fabric in a mute display of frustration.

'Come—come in,' he said weakly, lifting his hand to point at the tapestry-covered chair beside the bed. 'Do not look like that, *aghapitos*. I am not dying yet.'

Joanna came swiftly to the bed, but she didn't sit in the chair he'd indicated. Instead, she edged her hip onto the bed beside him, taking one of his hands between both of hers and gazing down at him with troubled eyes. 'Don't even suggest such a thing,' she reproved him sharply. Then, hesitatingly, 'Have you sent for a doctor?'

'What can a doctor do for me?' Constantine was dismissive. 'I am already sick of the cocktail of drugs I am forced to swallow every day, without inviting a handful more. No, Joanna, I have not sent for a doctor. A few hours' rest is all I need. Will you tell Demetri and Olivia that I am being lazy this morning?'

Joanna sighed. 'Shouldn't you tell them yourself?'

'And have them see me like this?' Constantine moved his head from side to side on the pillows. 'I know what they are like, Joanna. I would have no choice in the matter. Demetri would have Tsikas here immediately, and it is totally unnecessary.'

'Tsikas?' Joanna frowned. 'I assume he is your doctor.'

'He is the island doctor, yes,' agreed Constantine wearily. 'Look, Joanna, I do not wish to worry anyone. Livvy has enough to worry about, making the final preparations for Alex's wedding, and Demetri is already working flat out, trying to cope with my work as well as his own. Let him go on thinking that I am waiting for his explanation as to why two of my ships are not making me any money. Do not, I beg of you, put any doubts in their minds.'

Joanna shook her head. 'I don't think they'll like me making your excuses,' she said unhappily. 'But I take your point about worrying them unnecessarily. If it is unnecessarily,' she added doubtfully.

'It is.' Constantine was determined. 'You can tell Demetri I will speak with him this afternoon. I have taken my medication and in a few hours I should be as good as new.'

You wish, thought Joanna uneasily, but she knew better than to argue with him. Despite his physical weakness, Constantine's will was as strong as ever.

'All right?' he prompted when she didn't say anything, and Joanna gave a resigned shrug of her shoulders.

'I'll do what I can,' she promised, not looking forward to telling either of the Kastro offspring what their father had said. 'Now, get some rest, hmm?' She bent to bestow a warm kiss on his dry cheek. 'I'll come back at lunchtime to see how you are.'

Constantine nodded. 'We will have lunch together,' he said, patting her cheek. 'Oh, Joanna, how I wish I were twenty years younger. I would not be lying here like a beached whale while the woman I admire above all others was spending her time with my son instead of me.'

Joanna smiled, but as she got up from the bed she couldn't help thinking she'd bitten off more than she could chew by coming here. Yes, she cared about Constantine. Yes, it was easy to spend time with him. But dealing with his immediate family was another thing altogether. She supposed she had been naïve in imagining that they might welcome her into their midst, but she certainly hadn't expected them to be so openly hostile.

Though hostility was not what she had initially felt when Demetrios had surprised her on the terrace that morning. When he'd wrapped a towel about his nakedness—and she was pretty sure he had been swimming in the nude—and walked towards her, she'd felt a most unhostile surge of emotion. Indeed, for the first time in years she'd been physically aroused by a man's body. And although she'd later dismissed it as an aberration, now, faced with the prospect of confronting him again, Joanna knew she was apprehensive of the effect he had on her.

Philip was waiting for her outside the bedroom door. She wouldn't have been surprised if she'd discovered him with his ear pressed to the panels, but her exit had been sufficiently telegraphed to allow him time to move away.

'Mr Kastro is going to rest this morning,' she said coolly, deciding she was going to take no guff from him. 'I'll come back at one o'clock. Perhaps you'd ask the housekeeper to serve a light lunch on the balcony.'

Philip gave her a mutinous look. 'For one, *kiria*?'

'No, for two.'

She managed to keep her cool, but Philip wasn't finished yet. 'What would you like?' he asked, probably knowing full well that Joanna wasn't familiar with Greek food.

But she refused to let him confuse her. 'I suggest an omelette and some salad,' she answered sweetly. 'Mr Kastro is very fond of omelettes, you know?'

'*Veveha, kiria.* I know,' he muttered, as she headed towards her own rooms, and Joanna breathed a sigh of triumph as she closed the connecting doors behind her.

CHAPTER FOUR

DEMETRI was having breakfast on the terrace when Joanna appeared. At this hour of the morning the air outdoors was extremely pleasant, and the view from this elevated position never failed to lift his spirits.

And they'd needed lifting, he conceded grimly, picking at a currant-filled roll between generous gulps of the strong black coffee he favoured. His earlier encounter with his father's mistress had left him feeling piqued and morose. And provoked; definitely provoked. Though not in any way he wanted to acknowledge.

Now here she was again, slim and alluring in a sleeveless top and clinging silk shorts which had surely not come off the peg in some downtown department store. Her legs were bare and her glorious mane of hair had been secured in one of those loose knots atop her head. Strands of white-gold escaped to caress her cheeks, and although when she saw him she made a half-hearted effort to tuck them back behind her ears, they refused to be tamed.

Oh, she was beautiful, he thought bitterly, forced to push back his chair and get to his feet as she came towards him. But what the hell was she doing with his father? He simply didn't buy into May and December love affairs. She wanted something from this relationship, and he'd swear on a stack of Bibles that it wasn't sex.

The morning mail had been spread out on the table in front of him, but he shuffled it together at her approach. He guessed his father wouldn't be far behind her, and the last thing he wanted to do was talk about private business matters with her present.

He was pleased to see that she wasn't wholly relaxed about meeting him again. He wondered if she'd told Constantine about seeing him earlier that morning. If she had, he could probably look forward to his father's displeasure as well. Particularly if she'd mentioned that he'd been swimming in the nude.

Perhaps she hadn't noticed. After all, she hadn't noticed he was there at all until he'd vaulted out of the pool. Thank heaven for towels, he reflected drily. They could hide a multitude of sins.

'Mrs Manning,' he greeted her politely, inclining his head, and she managed a faint smile in return. But she was definitely antsy, and he decided to take pity on her. 'Are you and my father joining me for breakfast?'

'No,' Her denial was swift. But then, as if realising she had been a little hasty, she added, 'That is, your father won't be joining us.'

'Why not?' Demetri's eyes moved past her almost accusingly. 'Is something wrong?'

'He's—tired, that's all,' she told him quietly, apparently not knowing what to do with her hands. She finally folded them together over her midriff, inadvertently drawing his attention to the narrow strip of pale flesh exposed between her top and her shorts. 'He asked me to tell you he'll see you later today.'

Demetri's jaw clenched. He wasn't used to being given news about his father from a third party. He'd had to comply while his father was in the hospital, but being given information by a doctor was vastly different from hearing it from her.

'Are you sure you are telling me everything?' he asked, regarding her from beneath lowered lids, and he felt rather than saw the quiver of emotion that rippled over her at his question.

But, 'Of course,' she said quickly. Then, to his surprise, 'May I join you?'

Demetri frowned. 'Please,' he said without expression, but his thoughts were busy as she hurriedly seated herself in the chair across the table from his own. Was it only his imagination, or was this a deliberate attempt to divert him? He subsided again into his own chair. 'Have you eaten?'

'I—no.' She moistened her lips. 'But I'm not hungry. Perhaps I could have some coffee—'

She broke off as a white-aproned maid appeared at Demetri's elbow. The girl—for she was little more—gave her employer's son a proprietary smile before saying in their own language, 'Can I get you anything else, *kirie*?'

Demetri hesitated. And then, deciding that Mrs Manning couldn't be allowed to starve, he replied, 'Yes. Some toast and coffee for my guest, if you will? Thank you.'

The maid withdrew and Demetri, feeling a little more in command, lay back in his chair. *'Tora,'* he said pleasantly, 'perhaps you will now explain to me why my father is really not joining us for breakfast.'

A hint of colour entered her face. 'I've told you—'

'No.' His denial was soft but implacable. 'You have told me nothing. Are you saying he is not well enough to get out of bed?'

Her cheeks were definitely pink now. 'He said to tell you he was going to be lazy this morning,' she insisted. 'I've explained that he's feeling tired. The journey from England, yesterday's reception, and then dinner last night. He's not used to so much activity. Not—not all at once.'

'And entertaining a much younger woman?' suggested Demetri dangerously. 'Let us not forget your role in his recovery—or lack thereof. Whatever. Perhaps you are tiring him out, Mrs Manning.'

His words were unforgivable, and he knew a moment's remorse at his own cruelty. He had no excuse for blaming her for his father's weakness. Cancer didn't discriminate between its victims, and he should be grateful that she had brought the old man some comfort during his convalescence. Grateful, too, that to all intents and purposes his father had beaten the disease. And who knew that she hadn't had some part in that, as well?

Nevertheless, he despised himself for the sudden sympathy he felt when she turned her face away, blinking rapidly. She could be acting, of course, but he suspected he had upset her, and common sense told him that that was not the wisest thing to do. He had told Spiro he would handle this with kid gloves, but instead he was trampling finer feelings underfoot.

The return of the maid put an end to his self-admonishment. And if Joanna had been thinking of walking out on him, her actions were baulked by the serving woman setting a steaming pot of coffee and a linen-wrapped basket of toast at her elbow.

'*Afto ineh entaxi, kirie?*' Is that all right? the maid asked, looking at Demetri, and he drew a deep breath.

'*Ineh mia khara, efkharisto.*' It's fine, thanks, he responded, but Joanna was looking at him now, and she looked anything but pleased.

'Did you order this?' she demanded, uncaring that the maid was still standing beside the table, clearly understanding the tone of her voice, if not the words.

Demetri wasn't used to being embarrassed in front of his staff, and a muscle in his jaw jerked spasmodically as he strove to hide his anger. 'You have to eat something, Mrs Manning,' he said, aware that he no longer thought of her that way. Her first name was becoming far more familiar to him, and that was dangerous. '*Efkharisto*, Pilar. You may leave us.'

A gesture of his hand sent the young maid scurrying back into the villa, but he was going to have no such swift compliance from Joanna. 'I said I only wanted coffee,' she said, her blue eyes glittering now, her earlier emotion banished by a surge of indignation. 'I am not hungry, Mr Kastro. In fact, I can't think of anything I'd like less than sharing a meal with you!'

Demetri was outraged. 'You asked if you could join *me*, Mrs Manning,' he reminded her harshly, and her lips twisted in sudden distaste.

'That was a mistake,' she informed him, reaching for the pot of coffee and pouring herself a cup. Her hand was unsteady, he noticed, but he got little satisfaction from it. 'It was before I realised what a small-minded, selfish boor you are!'

Her voice was shaking by the time she'd finished, but with an admirable dignity she got to her feet. Then, picking up her coffee cup, she turned away, evidently intending to drink it in more congenial surroundings.

'Wait!' Despite the resentment he was feeling, Demetri was loath to let her go like this. '*Signomi,*' he said through clenched teeth. 'I am sorry. I did not mean to offend you.'

'No?' She'd paused, regarding him with scornful eyes. 'You virtually accuse me of exhausting your father with my demands and then try to tell me you didn't mean to offend me? Come on, Mr Kastro. Surely you can do better than that?'

Demetri breathed deeply. 'I spoke—without thinking,' he declared, but he could see from her expression that she didn't believe him.

'On the contrary,' she said, 'I think you knew exactly what you were saying. You might wish you hadn't exposed your feelings quite so openly, but that's all. Don't worry, Mr Kastro. I shan't tell your father what you said. I, at least, have more respect for him than that.'

She would have turned away then, but he moved swiftly round the table to detain her. 'All right,' he said tersely, aware that she was looking up at him now with a certain amount of apprehension. 'All right. You are right and I am wrong. It was a deliberate attempt to provoke you.' He paused. 'But, *Theos*, Joanna, you cannot have expected to come here without arousing some resentment.'

'Why not?' She blinked, and then said faintly, 'You called me Joanna. Was that another mistake?'

Demetri stifled an oath. 'No,' he said impatiently. Then, wearily, 'You must surely see that it is ludicrous for us to call one another Mrs Manning and Mr Kastro? My name is Demetri. Only my enemies call me Demetrios. And if we are to come to any kind of an understanding we should perhaps try and be civil with one another.'

Joanna hesitated. 'I notice you didn't suggest that we might be friends,' she remarked drily, but she was definitely thawing.

'Let us take each day at a time,' Demetri ventured, gesturing towards the breakfast table.

'Please. Will you sit with me?' He paused, and then added ruefully, 'My coffee is getting cold.'

She was reluctant, but her obvious desire to be accepted by her lover's family seemed to persuade her to give him a second chance. For his part, Demetri was grateful to have avoided an open rift between them. Despite the fact that even the thought of this woman and his father sharing a bed together filled him with revulsion, until he knew how much influence she had over the old man he would be wise not to make an enemy of her.

As if you could, a small voice inside him mocked contemptuously. Even knowing who she was and what she was doing didn't seem to make a scrap of difference to the unholy feelings she aroused inside him. However unscrupulous she might be, he wanted her. And that was something else he intended to change.

But, for now, she'd seated herself again and he was obliged to do the same. And there was no doubt that in other circumstances he would have enjoyed her company. She was good to look at, she made no demands on him, and her slightly husky voice gave everything she said a sensual intonation.

'This is a beautiful place,' she murmured after a few moments, and, acknowledging her effort to behave naturally, he gave a nod of assent.

'Beautiful, yes,' he agreed, his eyes lingering on her delicate profile. And then, when she sensed his regard and turned to look at him, 'My father built this house twenty-five years ago.'

'Twenty-five years?' She arched brows that were much darker than her hair. 'He must love the island very much.'

'It is where he was born,' remarked Demetri simply. 'Did he not tell you that?'

'No.' She bent her head to study the coffee in her cup. 'I suppose I assumed he'd been born in Athens.'

'Because his business was established there?'

'Maybe.'

'Or perhaps you think that Theapolis seems an unlikely place for a successful man to have his roots?'

Joanna looked up, her clear eyes mirroring a faint suspicion that his question hadn't been entirely innocent. 'We all have our roots somewhere, Mr—Demetri.' She paused. 'Even you.'

'And where are your roots, Joanna? London?'

'England, certainly,' she said evenly. Then, when he showed he expected her to go on, 'Actually, I was born in Norfolk. But my parents

were killed in an accident when I was quite young
and an elderly relative brought me up.'

He was surprised. Somehow he'd expected her
to have a different background. Or was he only
painting her with the brittle strokes of sophisti-
cation because it made it that much easier to despise her?

'Were you born on the island, too?' she asked,
when he didn't say anything, and Demetri gathered his thoughts.

'No,' he conceded flatly. 'I was born in Athens.
Olivia and me both. My younger sister, Alex, is
the only one of us who was born here.'

She inclined her head. 'Alex,' she said thoughtfully. 'I haven't met her yet.' She waited a beat.
'Is she like you?'

Demetri's eyes narrowed. 'In what way? In
looks? In temperament?'

'I suppose I meant, is she likely to resent me,
too?' observed Joanna quietly. 'What are you
afraid of, Demetri? I mean your father no harm.'

He was taken aback. He had never expected her
to broach her relationship with his father so
openly. But perhaps he had been naïve in thinking
he was in control. After all, he had always believed his father to be a shrewd judge of character, yet he had apparently been attracted to her.

She had infatuated him. Why should he be any different?

But he was!

'I do not know what you mean, Joanna,' he said now, his smile as guileless as his words. 'I understood we were to attempt a reconciliation.'

'A reconciliation—or an inquisition?' she demanded shortly. 'Why don't you come right out and ask me what you want to know?'

Demetri's lips twitched with reluctant amusement. 'I thought I was,' he admitted. Then, dispassionately, 'As to your enquiry about Alex, I think you will like her. She is nothing like Olivia, if that answers your question.'

'And you?'

'Me?' He pushed his cup aside and lay back in his chair. 'Modesty prevents me from making any comparisons.'

'Really?'

Joanna was sceptical, and he felt a momentary dislike of his own duplicity. What he would have really liked to do today was to go sailing and escape the machinations of both his father and his mistress. It was weeks, *months*, since he had had a completely free day, and although he knew he was being selfish in thinking this way when his father had been so ill, he was only human.

His eyes were drawn towards the jetty where the sailboat rocked at anchor and, as if sensing his frustration, Joanna murmured, 'Whose boat is that?' in a different, gentler tone.

'She is mine,' Demetri responded, with some satisfaction. 'The *Circe*. She is a two-masted schooner, but one person can handle her with ease.'

'And you do?' she prompted, and he was aware of her eyes on him rather than the yacht.

'When I can,' he conceded, turning to meet her gaze and surprising a faintly envious expression on her face. He considered for a moment, and then added, 'Do you sail?'

'Unfortunately not.' Her eyes moved to the sailboat again. 'I envy you. Where I used to live when I was young, people sailed dinghies. Nothing as sophisticated as your boat, of course. But it looked fun.'

'The Broads,' he said, after a moment, and she was startled into looking at him again.

'You know Norfolk?'

'I spent a year backpacking around Europe,' he told her lightly. 'Naturally I spent some time in England. Then, later, I spent a year at the London School of Economics.'

'The LSE?' She was obviously surprised. 'Did you enjoy your time there?'

'I liked London.' Demetri realised he was in danger of becoming too familiar with her. 'Small world.'

'Isn't it?' She hesitated for a moment, and then said, 'You know, I think I will have a slice of toast, after all. Do you mind?'

Demetri could think of few things he'd like less at this moment than to sit here and watch her consume her breakfast. To see those even white teeth digging into the toast, to observe the delicate tip of her tongue emerging to lick a crumb of bread from the corner of that luscious mouth: that was the stuff of fantasy and he wanted no part of it. But civility demanded that he at least ensure that what she ate was hot, so he glanced round, saying quickly, 'I will have Pilar bring you some fresh—'

'No!'

Her denial was instantaneous, and accompanied by an instinctive reaching for his arm to prevent him from raising it to summon the maid. He was less formally dressed this morning, and his cotton tee shirt left his arm bare. In consequence, her fingers brushed across his flesh with devastating effect.

Her touch seemed to burn his skin, but he knew it was just his own unwelcome attraction to her that caused the sensation. Those cool, slim fingers couldn't burn anything, but that didn't prevent an answering flame of awareness from spreading along his veins like wildfire.

The blood surged to the surface of his skin and it was all he could do not to act upon the impulses that had him in their grip. The desire to stretch out his hand, loop it around her nape and bring that parted tantalising mouth to his was almost overwhelming. He could almost taste her sweetness; almost feel the softness of her lips and the satisfying invasion of his tongue. His eyes dropped to her breasts and saw, as if through a haze, the hard nubs straining at the cloth. *Theos*, he thought dizzily, if he didn't get out of here soon he was going to do something he'd definitely regret.

Thrusting back his chair, he got abruptly to his feet. Escape, he though unsteadily. Like everything else in life, escape was relative. He'd imagined his only escape was in getting away from his responsibilities, but it wasn't true. Now, he knew, he needed quite desperately to get away from her.

'As you wish,' he said politely, as if all he'd been thinking about was her satisfaction. He pushed slightly unsteady fingers through his hair. 'And now I am afraid I must leave you. Spiro will be waiting for me. If you do change your mind about the food, Pilar will be more than happy to serve you.'

CHAPTER FIVE

'TO SERVE *you*,' muttered Joanna under her breath as he walked away. She'd seen the way the young maid had looked at Demetri, and the hunger she'd exhibited had been unmistakable. She wondered if he practised *droit de seigneur* with the female staff, and then scoffed at the thought. It was sour grapes. She didn't even like him, but that didn't stop her from being aware of him in a purely sexual way.

She scowled, suddenly losing all taste for the toast she'd put on her plate. She couldn't be attracted to him, sexually or otherwise, she told herself severely. The man despised her, for God's sake, and he made little effort to hide it. He'd been civil to her this morning, but she didn't delude herself that he was doing it for anyone other than his father. And she'd agreed to come here for Constantine's sake, she reminded herself. How convincing would their relationship seem if she allowed herself to be seduced by his son?

But that wouldn't happen. She didn't want another man in her life, period. She was twenty-six, but in terms of experience she sometimes felt she was twenty years older. Which made her a suitable companion for Demetri's father. He had thought so, and, what was more, he wouldn't make any demands on her that she couldn't fulfil.

A shiver slid down her spine and she gave herself a little shake to dispel it. How long was it going to take her to put her marriage to Richard out of her head? Occasionally she had the depressing feeling that it would never happen.

A soft breeze blew up from the water, cooling the damp tendrils of hair that clung to her temple, bringing a reassuring wave of awareness of where she was and why she was there. Constantine wouldn't approve of her sitting here feeling sorry for herself. He wanted her to enjoy this trip. Apart from what he'd asked of her, he'd wanted to give her a holiday to remember—an opportunity to escape once and for all from the psychological walls she'd built around herself.

And she would enjoy it, she assured herself, reaching for the butter and spreading it thickly over the now cold toast. She was not going to let the young Kastros spoil it for her. She was tougher than that. She had had to be. And the sooner they realised it, the better.

To her dismay, Constantine was weaker at lunchtime.

She had spent the morning avoiding any further

confrontations with members of his family, but when she presented herself at the doors to his suite at a little after twelve, Philip let her in with a decidedly anxious look on his face.

'Khriazomasteh enan yatro, kiria,' he exclaimed as soon as the door was closed behind her. *'Stenokhori-emeh!'*

Joanna made a helpless gesture. 'I'm sorry—' she began blankly, and to her relief Philip seemed to understand.

'A doctor, kiria,' he said urgently. 'We need a doctor. Kirie Constantine—*ineh arostos, kiria*. He is—ill!'

Joanna pressed an anxious hand to her throat. 'Why do you say that?' she demanded in an undertone, glancing towards Constantine's bedroom door, which was, mercifully, closed. 'What's happened?'

Philip shook his head. 'I have—I know Kirie Constantine *pola*—many—years, *kiria*. He—he sleeps—too much.'

'He's tired,' protested Joanna, not altogether convinced she was right, and Philip waved an impatient hand.

'I think we ask Kirie Demetri, *kiria*. He know what to do, *ne*?'

'*Ne*. I mean, *okhi*.' Joanna remembered just in time that *ne* meant yes and not no, which was what it sounded like. 'That is,' she continued, trying to think, 'is that what Kirie Constantine said?'

'*Then katalaveno, kiria.*'

Philip looked mutinous and Joanna suspected he knew exactly what she'd said. 'Have you spoken with Kirie Constantine?' she persisted, speaking slowly so he had no excuse for saying he didn't understand, and the manservant shrugged.

'*Okhi, kiria,*' he said offhandedly, and she hoped he wasn't going to insist on speaking Greek. Then, with a slight softening of his expression, 'I tell you, *kiria*. He sleep all the time.'

Joanna tried not to feel too anxious. Ever since Constantine had got out of hospital he had spent much of the day resting. And, as she'd thought earlier, yesterday had been a particularly strenuous day for a man in his condition. Especially as it had followed on from another tiring day. It was surely reasonable that he was sleeping. It was probably the best thing for him.

But...

'I think I'd better see for myself,' she declared, hoping she sounded more confident than she felt. Then, not really caring whether Philip had understood her or not, she crossed the room to Constantine's bedroom door. 'Give me a few minutes,' she said, opening the door. 'Then I'll speak to you again.'

'*Ne, kiria.*'

Philip shrugged again, turning his head away, but she felt him watching her out of the corners of his eyes as she went into Constantine's room. She sighed. She supposed the man had a right to his feelings. He had known his employer a lot longer than she had.

She closed the door behind her, mostly to prevent the uneasy sense that Philip was peering over her shoulder, and approached the bed. Constantine had his eyes closed, but as she looked down at him they opened, and she took an involuntary step backwards, ashamed to admit that she'd allowed the manservant's words to spook her.

'Hi,' she said, the word coming out a little higher than normal, and squeaky. 'How—how are you?'

'I have to confess I am a little more weary than I anticipated,' Constantine answered her ruefully. 'I am sorry. What time is it?'

Joanna inched her hip onto the bed and took his hand. 'It's about half past twelve,' she said. 'Do you want some lunch?'

'Lunch?' Constantine's expression was revealing, but he quickly hid his revulsion. 'Oh, Joanna, my dear, I do not think I am very hungry just now.'

'That's all right.' Joanna squeezed his hand reassuringly. 'You just take things easy. Have you had your medication? Is there anything I can get for you?'

Constantine shook his head. 'I am fine, really,' he insisted, though it was obvious he was not. 'In a couple of hours I will be up and about again. But I am afraid we will have to postpone our outing until tomorrow.'

'No problem,' said Joanna, wishing she felt more confident about the situation. She hesitated, and then added persuasively. 'Wouldn't you like me to tell Demetri—?'

'Nothing!' For the first time since she'd entered the room, Constantine looked positively animated. 'I want you to promise me you will tell Demetri nothing. If he knew—if he were to suspect that I have not made a full recovery, he would cancel the wedding. I know my son, Joanna. He is a good man, and I love him, but in this instance I will not allow him to treat me as an invalid and destroy Alex's happiness.'

Joanna was very much afraid that Alex's happiness would be destroyed anyway, when she discovered what was wrong with her father, but she couldn't argue with Constantine now.

Nevertheless, she couldn't help feeling a certain amount of sympathy for Demetri. However self-less Constantine thought he was being, his children were going to be devastated when they found out the truth.

'He—I think he's expecting to speak to you this afternoon,' she ventured, remembering how insulting Demetri had been about her role in Constantine's recovery. 'He's bound to ask me what's going on. He wasn't very happy with my explanation this morning.'

'Then you will have to improvise,' declared Constantine wearily. 'Come, Joanna. I am sure you can think of some way to divert my son from becoming suspicious.' He paused, his thin lips twisting a little bitterly. 'Use your imagination.'

Joanna stared at him 'I hope you're not asking me to—'

'No. No.' Once again Constantine grew restless beneath her gaze. 'I would not do that. I meant—' He considered. 'Ask him to take you to see the ruins of Athena's temple. Demetri is quite well-versed in the history of the area, and the temple is the highest point on the island. The view is—' He broke off, his energy depleted. 'I am sorry,' he said again. 'I so much wanted to show you my island.'

'You will,' insisted Joanna encouragingly, squeezing his dry fingers once more. She got to her feet, making no promises about asking Demetri anything. 'I'll come back later, when you're feeling more rested.' She smiled, kissing her fingertips and pressing them to his forehead. 'I do care about you, Constantine. I hope you know that.'

He smiled then, but his eyes had closed, and although the smile lingered on his lips she could tell he'd lost consciousness again. Anxiety gripped her. She felt so ill equipped to handle this situation. It was an enormous responsibility Constantine had placed on her, and when Demetri found out—

She decided to have lunch on the balcony. Faithful to her instructions, however unwillingly, Philip was waiting to serve the salad and omelettes she'd ordered when she emerged from Constantine's room. Her explanation that his employer would be getting up later met with a sceptical stare, but the manservant knew better than to argue with her again. Instead, he obediently attended to her needs, ensuring she had everything necessary with polite deference.

And she had, she thought after he'd gone, seating herself at the table and cupping her chin in one hand as she stared at the view. How could anyone find fault with this place? It was heavenly.

A basket of crusty bread accompanied the meal, together with bottles of both wine and water to assuage her thirst. Salad, crisp and green, and liberally threaded with sliced avocados, peppers and olives, nestled in an ice-cooled container, and golden-brown omelettes rested beneath a heated dome.

Turning her attention to the food, Joanna did her best to enjoy it, but she'd spent most of the morning in a state of raw anxiety and nothing Constantine had said had eased her conscience.

Nevertheless, she was hungry, and, ensconced here on the balcony, she felt reassuringly secure from either Demetri or Olivia's wrath. They were bound to want to speak to her later, but for the moment she was determined not to let thoughts of them spoil her appetite.

Not that she ever ate a lot, she conceded, picking at a curl of lettuce. It was many years since she'd had the kind of appetite that would have done justice to the meal. She supposed she was lucky that she had the sort of metabolism that meant she could eat what she liked without gaining any weight, but not since she was a schoolgirl had she really looked forward to her food.

But then that was all tied up with her parents being killed in an avalanche in Austria and going to live with her father's maiden aunt, who had had little time for a spirited youngster. Meals in Aunt Ruth's house had hardly been happy occasions, with the old lady constantly bemoaning the fact that what little money she had was scarcely enough for her to live on, let alone provide for a gangling girl who was always growing out of her shoes and clothes.

Joanna, at first grief-stricken and confused, had soon learned that life was never going to be the same again, and by the time she was sixteen she had already been planning what she was going to do when she left school. College or university had been out of the question; she'd known that. Her aunt would have said they couldn't afford it. Besides, she'd had no desire to be any more of a burden to her aunt, financially or otherwise. Only the knowledge that her parents would have been horrified if she'd insisted on leaving school after her GCSEs had persuaded her to stay on until she'd taken the higher exams.

At eighteen, however, she'd been more than ready to find a job and start supporting herself. But once again fate had intervened. Her aunt had had a stroke, which meant that Joanna had had no choice but to go on living with her and caring for her. For the next four years she had been her aunt's nurse, eking out an existence on the little money the social services provided.

It wasn't until the old lady died that Joanna had discovered the trust that her father had set up for her. For years the money had been collecting interest in a fund which should have been used to pay for her personal needs and her education. But her aunt had chosen not to use it or tell her about it. Instead she'd let the girl think that her parents had left her penniless as well as alone.

Why she'd done it, Joanna had no idea. Perhaps she had been an embittered old spinster, as the solicitor had said. In any event, after her aunt's death Joanna had sold the small semi where she'd spent the last ten years of her life and bought herself a comfortable apartment in Kensington. She'd splurged on a new wardrobe, had her long hair cut and styled, and finally taken a holiday in Sardinia. Where she'd met Richard Manning...

A shadow crossed the sun and she pushed her plate away. Then, sliding her legs to the side, she got up from her chair and crossed to the balcony rail. Resting her hands on the hot metal, she tried to dispel the feelings of inadequacy that remembering the months she'd spent with Richard caused her. But she was always amazed at her own naïvety. Had she never suspected that he was not what he seemed?

Apparently not, she thought bitterly. At twenty-two, she'd been less sexually aware than a girl slightly more than half her age. She'd never had a regular boyfriend. Aunt Ruth had not encouraged her to see her friends outside school. And, because she'd succeeded in instilling a sense of obligation in the girl, Joanna had always felt that she couldn't let her aunt down.

Which was also why Richard had made such a positive impression on her. Tall and fair and good-looking, with a background of public school and an excellent job in the City, he'd seemed everything she could ever have wished for in a man. The fact that he'd been on holiday with another man hadn't seemed so unusual. He'd seemed suave and sophisticated, and she'd been incredibly flattered when he'd singled her out for attention.

The holiday had been everything she'd ever hoped for. Richard had spent much of his time with her, taking her out in the car he'd hired, dining with her at all the best restaurants. When she'd mentioned the fact that he was neglecting his friend he'd insisted that it didn't matter. He wanted to be with her, he'd said disarmingly, and she'd had no reason not to believe him.

She'd been thrilled when he'd phoned her after they'd got back to London. She'd been half afraid it had just been a holiday friendship, and that she'd been too inexperienced to hold the attention of a man like him. The fact that so far he hadn't even attempted to kiss her had made her doubt his feelings for her, but when she'd voiced as much to Richard he'd assured her it was because he had too much respect for her as a woman.

Joanna's lips twisted now. Even with the sun beating down on her shoulders she felt cold. Respect! She doubted if Richard even knew the meaning of the word. He'd used her, that was all. He'd had his own agenda, and she'd just been his pawn.

Unable and unwilling to continue with this train of thought, Joanna left the balcony and went back inside. But the beauty of her sitting room was of little comfort to her and, deciding she needed to escape, she fled the room and went downstairs.

As she crossed the marble foyer she heard voices coming from the terrace. She guessed Demetri and Olivia, and possibly Spiro Stavros as well, were having lunch outdoors, and she envied them their freedom to do as they liked. They were speaking in their own language, so she didn't understand what they were saying, but in any case she didn't want to be accused of eavesdropping so she quickened her step.

'Mrs Manning!'

She'd reached the door which led out onto the crushed shell forecourt at the front of the villa when Demetri's voice arrested her. She didn't know why she recognised his voice so instinctively, but she did, and, although she was tempted to pretend she hadn't heard him, courtesy demanded that she acknowledge his presence.

In the few seconds it took her to come to this decision, however, he had covered the space between them, and when he spoke again his warm breath fanned her neck.

'Joanna.' He had evidently remembered they were supposed to have called a truce. 'Where are you going? Where is my father?'

Joanna turned reluctantly, remembering all too well how disturbing she'd found him earlier in the day. And although she had other things on her mind—not least the memory of how Richard had deceived her—she was instantly conscious of Demetri's dark attraction and the warm male scent of his body.

'I—I thought I might go for a walk,' she said spontaneously, not really knowing until that moment what she'd had in mind. 'It's such a lovely day.'

'And much too hot to venture out without any protection,' observed Demetri drily, raising his hand as if to check that her bare arms were free of any sunscreen and then thrusting it into the pocket of his drawstring pants. 'You do not even have a hat.'

'I don't intend to go far,' said Joanna, realising belatedly that she hadn't thought it through. She was so used to England, so used to cool breezes even in September, that she hadn't stopped to consider the wisdom of her decision.

'You are going alone?' Demetri was persistent. 'My father is not going with you?'

'No.' Once again Joanna was conscious of being between a rock and a hard place. 'I think your father needs to take things easy today. He—er— he apologises for his tardiness. He's not going to make your meeting after all.'

Demetri frowned. 'You have seen him, I assume?'

Joanna's cheeks turned a little pink. 'Of course.'

'Of course.' Demetri's mouth lifted slightly in faint contempt. 'How could I doubt it? He appears to have put all his trust in you.'

'Hardly that.' Joanna couldn't let him go on thinking they were conducting some kind of intimate liaison, particularly when she was already worried that Constantine wasn't responding to his treatment as he should. 'He's just weary, that's all. I think he needs a complete rest.'

Demetri studied her in silence for a moment, and she had the uneasy feeling that he could see right through her. She hoped not. Right now, she didn't think she could cope with another confrontation.

'You have not called a doctor?' he asked at last, and Joanna sighed. She should have known this was coming.

'No,' she said. 'He doesn't want to see a doctor. He has his medication.' She crossed her arms across her midriff. 'That should be enough.'

'You have made that decision?' he enquired tersely, and again she wished Constantine hadn't put her in this position.

'No. He has,' she insisted doggedly. Then, finding inspiration, 'You know your father. He will not take advice from anyone.'

'That is true.' To her relief, Demetri seemed to accept her explanation. 'So that is why you are— how do you put it?—at a loose end?'

Joanna lifted her shoulders. 'No,' she answered, not altogether truthfully. 'I—just thought it would be pleasant to get out of the house.'

'So you decided to go for a walk in the midday sun?'

She glanced at her watch. 'It's hardly midday.'

'The two o'clock sun, then,' he amended. 'Though the distinction escapes me. It is just as hot now as it was earlier. May I recommend that you confine your activities to the villa until later in the afternoon?'

Joanna expelled a weary breath. 'Is that an order?'

Demetri's mouth compressed. 'It is the advice of someone who knows this climate perhaps a little better than you do,' he told her flatly. 'I would not like you to suffer sunstroke. It is what my father would say if he were here. I am sure he would expect me to look after his—his friend.'

Joanna gave in. 'All right,' she said. 'I'll go back to my room.'

'Or you could sit beside the pool,' suggested Demetri, gesturing towards the terrace. 'There are umbrellas there to protect you.'

No, thanks, Joanna thought, not willing to lay herself open to any more questions. But she didn't say it. Instead, she gave Demetri a polite smile and, without giving him an answer, walked swiftly away towards the stairs.

CHAPTER SIX

DEMETRI went to see his father in the late afternoon.

He hadn't seen Joanna since he'd spoken to her just after lunch, and although he couldn't altogether blame her for wanting to avoid the other members of his family, he was irritated that she had chosen to spend the afternoon in her room.

Na pari i oryi. He'd been civil to her, hadn't he? More than civil when he considered how frustrated she made him feel. It might not be her fault that he had a physical reaction every time he was near her, but, *Theos*, it wasn't his either. His father should never have brought her here. Couldn't he see what kind of woman she was? Didn't he realise that she knew exactly how men responded to her sexuality, how she must have used her experience to infatuate him?

Philip let him into his father's apartments. The old manservant seemed relieved to see him, and Demetri guessed Philip wasn't finding the situation any easier than he was. But, remembering the *faux pas* he had made the last time he was here, Demetri paused in the doorway to the salon, looking about him intently before venturing any further.

'Mrs Manning?' he said, glancing towards his father's bedroom door. His stomach clenched. 'Is she here?'

'No, *kirie*.' Philip twisted his hands together. 'I have not seen her since before lunch.'

Demetri breathed a little more easily. 'And my father?'

'Your father, *kirie*?' Philip looked confused. 'His condition is unchanged.'

'His condition?' Demetri stiffened. 'What condition?'

Philip shifted a little nervously. 'But surely you know, *kirie*? Kiria Manning—'

He broke off, as if afraid he was saying too much, but Demetri wouldn't let him avoid an answer. 'Yes?' he demanded. 'Kiria Manning— what? What has she been keeping from me?'

Philip looked uncomfortable now. 'I do not know what Kiria Manning has told you, *kirie*, but your father is not well. He has spent most of the day sleeping.'

'Oh.' Demetri made a dismissive gesture. 'I know that. Mrs Manning says that he is tired, that the activities of the last two days have been too much for him. Rest is what he needs.'

'He has eaten nothing, *kirie*.' Philip was defensive. 'He was going to have lunch with Kiria Manning, but she was forced to dine alone.'

Demetri frowned. 'Are you sure?'

'I served her myself,' said Philip stiffly. 'Did she not tell you?'

Joanna had told him nothing beyond the fact that his father was weary, thought Demetri impatiently, resenting anew this feeling of being excluded from his father's affairs. But he had no intention of telling Philip that.

'She may have said something,' he said now, hiding his real feelings. Then, determinedly, 'Is he awake?'

'I do not know, *kirie*.' Philip wasn't a fool and he had detected Demetri's unwillingness to confide in a servant. 'Perhaps you should ask Kiria Manning.'

Demetri's dark eyes bored into the old man's. 'You said she was not here.'

'She is not here.' Philip could be awkward, too. 'I merely meant—'

'I think I know what you meant, Philip,' Demetri interrupted him drily. 'I am disappointed in you. I would have expected you to inform me of any deterioration in my father's condition, not Kiria Manning.'

Philip gave him a wounded look, but before either of them could act on their feelings the door to Constantine's bedroom opened and the man himself appeared in the aperture.

'What is going on here?' he demanded, and Demetri was overwhelmingly relieved to see that his father was apparently capable of standing up for himself. 'Demetri? What are you doing here? I asked Joanna to tell you I would see you later.'

Demetri stared at the old man in some frustration. Was it only his imagination, or perhaps the white towelling of his bathrobe that gave his thin face an unnatural pallor? Whatever, now was not the time to take umbrage at anything he said and, forcing a tight smile, he gave a slight bow of his head.

'I was concerned that you could not keep our appointment, Papa,' he replied evenly. 'That is all.'

'But Joanna—'

'Mrs Manning explained that you were—exhausted—after your journey,' Demetri agreed, realising how much easier this would be if 'Joanna' did not continually come between them. 'But I am your son. Do I not deserve the same courtesy as—as your friend?'

Constantine's features seemed to hollow and weariness etched every line of his face. 'Of course,' he said, and now Demetri noticed he was supporting himself with one hand against the frame of the door. 'I am sorry, *mi yos*. Please.' He glanced over his shoulder into the room behind him. 'Come in.'

Demetri exchanged a look with Philip. '*Poli kala*, if you are sure?'

Constantine's thin lips twitched. 'As you say, Demetri, you are my son. My successor, *okhi*? How can I deny you a few minutes of my time?'

Demetri hesitated, but then, after asking Philip to bring them some refreshment, he followed his father into the bedroom. His bedroom? he wondered, his tension mounting as the old man climbed with evident relief back onto the wide bed. Or theirs? He felt impatience grip him. No, dammit, he would not think of that now. Joanna Manning had her own apartments. He should know. Wasn't that where he had found them together?

'So, Demetri...' Constantine's expression had eased a little now that he was resting more comfortably. 'As you can see, I am not yet as strong as I would wish to be. But it will come. Given time.'

Demetri positioned himself at the end of the bed. 'We are all praying for that day, Papa,' he said huskily 'And, if it is of any comfort to you,

Kastro International is in safe hands, whatever Nikolas Poros says.'

'I am sure.' His father gave a rueful smile. 'I have great faith in you, Demetri. I know you will never do anything to let me or—or your sisters down.'

Demetri blew out a breath. 'I am glad to hear it.'

'Did you doubt it?'

'Well…'

Demetri hesitated. He could hardly say that since Joanna Manning had come on the scene he was finding it increasingly difficult to be sure of anything.

'Oh, I know it has not always been easy for you, Demetri,' his father went on, evidently misunderstanding his silence. 'And had things been different you would have had a brother—brothers—to share the burden with you. But…' He sighed. 'Regrettably, your mother was not strong, and having Alexandra was simply too much for her.'

'I know that, Papa.' Demetri felt uneasy suddenly. It was as if Constantine was already preparing him for the day when he wouldn't be around to share the burden himself. 'I just wanted you to know—'

The sound of the door opening across the room allowed him a moment to collect his thoughts, but when he turned his head he saw it wasn't Philip who had interrupted them. Joanna had paused in the doorway. Her face flushed with anger or concern, he couldn't be sure which, and she advanced swiftly into the room. She gave him a glowering look before halting beside the bed and taking one of his father's hands between both of hers. Then, in a voice that was filled with an emotion he didn't care to identify, she said, 'What's going on, Constantine? Is—is Demetri supposed to be here?'

Demetri's indignation was instantaneous. 'What are you implying, Mrs Manning?' he exclaimed, forgetting that earlier in the day he had practically demanded that they use one another's first names. 'I would do nothing to endanger my father's health.'

'*Siopi, siopi!*' Quiet, quiet! Constantine heaved a weary sigh. 'Joanna, my dear, there is no need for you to defend me so diligently. And—' he turned to Demetri '—you must forgive Joanna, *mi ghios*. She has only my best interests at heart.'

'As do we all, Papa,' said Demetri fiercely, resenting having to say it yet again. His shoulders stiffened. 'Would you like me to go?'

'No, no.' His father lifted his free hand and then let it fall again. 'Not like this.' He looked at the woman who had now eased her hip onto the bed beside him. 'Joanna, I want you and Demetri to be friends. Not enemies. Please.' Demetri saw the veins in his wrist stand out in stark relief as he squeezed her hand. 'For my sake.'

Demetri said nothing as Joanna turned to look at him again, but he guessed she hid her own resentment from the old man. 'Um—Demetri and I are not enemies, Constantine,' she assured him, squeezing his hand in her turn. Her slim arms were faintly tinged with red and Demetri guessed she had spent at least part of the afternoon on her balcony. He also noticed that she did not say that they were *friends*. That would have been too much, even for her.

'I am glad,' his father said now, but Demetri could see he was visibly weakening. How long was it since he had had any sustenance? He wished he could remember what the old man had eaten at dinner the night before, but he had been so incensed by Joanna's presence that he had paid little attention to details like that.

'I think we should go,' he said abruptly, and once again Joanna turned a cool gaze in his direction.

'Yes, you should,' she agreed, her deep blue eyes calm and dismissive. 'Your father needs to rest.'

'You are not his nurse, Joanna,' he responded, keeping his temper with an effort. 'I think we should both leave my father to Philip's ministrations, *ne*?'

Joanna hesitated. She was obviously torn by the desire to find out what he and his father had been talking about and the knowledge that for once he might have a point.

With an obvious effort she got up from the bed, still retaining her hold on his father's hand as she said, 'Is that what you want, Constantine?'

'It might be for the best, *agapi mou*,' he conceded gently, but as Demetri started for the door his father's voice detained him. '*Avrio,*' he said. Tomorrow. 'If I am still—what can I say? Incapacitated, no?—will you look after Joanna?'

'There's no need,' she began at once, but Constantine was looking at his son and Demetri didn't have the heart to refuse him.

'*Veveha*, Papa.' Of course. Demetri inclined his head, his lips twisting with reluctant irony. 'It will be my pleasure.'

To her relief, Philip informed Joanna the next morning that his employer had swallowed a little soup at suppertime. According to the old man Constantine had had a reasonably good night, and she began to hope that the fears she had entertained the day before might be only that: fears. After all, Constantine's doctors would not have allowed him to return to Theapolis if they had suspected the journey would be too much for him.

Joanna, herself, had spent a less than peaceful night. Despite the fact that Demetri had been painfully polite to her during and after the dinner she had been obliged to share with him and his family the evening before, the prospect of spending any time in his company was daunting. Had she even suspected Constantine might deputise his son to act as his proxy, she would have made sure he knew exactly how she felt about it. As it was, he'd sprung the request on both of them, and she doubted Demetri was any more pleased by the arrangement than she was.

Not that she really knew what Demetri thought about anything. He was far too clever at hiding his feelings for that. Just occasionally, when he looked at her, she had the sense that what he felt towards her was more than just dislike. Did he hate her? Did he hate the fact that his father cared about her? Or did he simply hate what he thought she was? Whatever, she wasn't looking forward to having him as an unwilling companion.

Perhaps she should have asked him to send Spiro in his place, she reflected, checking her appearance in the long mirrors in her dressing room. Not that she knew him any better, but she suspected he might be easier to get along with. As it was, having seen Constantine and assured herself that he was feeling much better this morning, she'd been forced to accept that he was still not well enough to look after her himself. She was therefore committed to spending the morning with a man she neither liked nor trusted, and she wished she had something in her wardrobes that didn't proclaim her sex quite so blatantly.

Still, she couldn't deny that it was good to wear attractive clothes again, and although the cream linen pants clung to the feminine curve of her hip and thigh, at least her legs were covered. But at what expense? Would Demetri understand that the buttoned waistcoat top that went with the trousers was meant to expose an inch or two of lightly tanned midriff every time she moved, or would he imagine she had chosen the most suggestive outfit she could find?

Either way, she refused to worry about that now. Constantine had suggested she should eat breakfast downstairs this morning, instead of skulking in her room. Of course he hadn't used those words, but Joanna knew what he'd meant.

He was trying to integrate her into the life of the household, and, however she might feel about it, she owed it to him to go along with his wishes.

To her relief, the terrace was deserted. If Constantine's son and daughter had had breakfast there they were long gone, and only a few crumbs in the centre of the white cloth betrayed that a basket of bread had sat there. A place had been laid at the table overlooking the gardens that fell away towards the beach, and, although Joanna's appetite hardly warranted such a formal arrangement, she pulled out the chair and sat down.

Almost immediately the maid, Pilar, arrived to serve her, and by means of the odd word and quite a lot of sign language Joanna managed to convey her needs to her. The coffee was easy enough; everyone apparently had coffee at breakfast. But the milk and cornflakes were harder. How did you mime the difference between a bowl of muesli and the world's most famous brand of cereal?

'She understands English, you know,' remarked a lazy voice Joanna was beginning to recognise only too well as Pilar sauntered away. Demetri, who had apparently been watching her from the wide glass doors that opened onto the terrace, now strolled towards her. 'Do not be surprised if you get offered porridge instead.'

Joanna pursed her lips. 'If you knew that, why didn't you say so?' she demanded sharply, and then struggled to contain her anger. 'That is—how long have you been standing there, watching me?'

'Long enough,' remarked Demetri indifferently, moving past her to prop his hips against the low wall that edged the terrace. 'How are you this morning? How is my father?'

'Don't you know?'

Once again Joanna found it difficult to be civil with him. Whatever he said, whatever he did, seemed inclined to rub her up the wrong way, and she was fairly sure it was deliberate.

'Obviously not,' he responded mildly now. 'You are his mistress, Joanna. Do you not know?'

'I'm not—' Joanna had to bite her tongue to prevent her anger from betraying her. She licked her lips and began again. 'I'm not—an expert,' she improvised. 'But I think he's a little better.'

'I am relieved to hear it.'

Demetri accepted her reply at face value, lifting one canvas-shod foot to rest vertically against the low wall. It drew her attention to the fact that he was wearing dark blue shorts this morning, and she hated herself for noticing the powerful length of muscular leg that they displayed. Legs that were lightly covered with the same night-dark

hair that sprang from the open neck of his collar-
less cotton shirt and framed the narrow gold
watch that circled his wrist. Much against her
will, she found herself speculating about the rest
of his body, imagining how his skin would feel
beneath her—oh, God!—sweating palms.

'So what would you like to do?'

'To do?' With an effort Joanna dragged her
thoughts back from the precipice of her imagination and gazed at him blankly. 'I don't know
what you—'

'This morning?' prompted Demetri. 'I thought
you might like to take a drive around the island.'
He pushed his hands into the pockets of his
shorts, drawing the cloth taut across his thighs. 'I
could show you the ruins of the temple of Athena
that dates back to the fourth century B.C.'

'A temple?' Joanna surreptitiously dried her
hands on the knees of her trousers and concen-
trated on the logo on his shirt. Anything to avoid
looking anywhere else. 'Well, I—you don't have
to entertain me, you know.'

'I want to,' he said, straightening up from the
wall. 'Ah, here is Pilar with your breakfast.'

Joanna turned her head to watch the maid's approach, convinced that she wouldn't be able to
eat anything with Demetri looking over her shoulder—metaphorically speaking. Her throat felt un-

pleasantly dry, and it wasn't just the fact that she hadn't had anything to drink yet. What did he really want? she wondered. Why was he being so nice to her? Was it just because his father had asked him to, or did he have some hidden agenda of his own?

Despite Joanna's fears, Pilar had evidently decided it would be unwise to pretend ignorance with Demetri on hand to take exception to any provocation on her part. On the tray she set down on the table were the milk and cornflakes Joanna had requested, along with a jug of freshly squeezed orange juice, a rack of toast, and a pot of coffee. And *two* cups, Joanna noted tensely. Apparently she was supposed to invite Demetri to join her.

'*Ineh entaxi, kiria?*' asked Pilar politely, and, despite Joanna's limited knowledge of Greek, she understood enough to know that the girl was asking for her approval.

'It's—fine. Thank you,' she said, reaching eagerly for the orange juice and pouring some into a glass. She took a grateful sip. 'Delicious.'

'*Efkharistisi mou, kiria,*' responded the maid, her dark eyes seeking Demetri's endorsement, too. '*Tha itheles tipoteh alo?*'

'Nothing else,' responded Demetri briefly. 'You can go.'

Pilar's mouth turned down, but she turned obediently away and Joanna was left with the awkward dilemma of not knowing what to do for the best. If Demetri was being friendly for a change she would be unwise to oppose it. On the other hand, she was far too aware that he was a dangerous man in more ways than one.

But to her relief the decision wasn't left to her. 'I will leave you to have your breakfast in peace,' he said, and she wondered with a sense of unease if he could read her thoughts. 'I suggest we meet again at—' he glanced at his watch '—half past nine, *ne*?'

Joanna licked a smear of orange juice from her lower lip. It didn't sound as if she was being given a lot of choice. 'I—all right,' she said, wishing she didn't sound so submissive. 'Thank you.'

'There is no need for you to thank me, Joanna,' he replied, his dark eyes narrowed and impenetrable. 'I shall—look forward to it.'

Yeah, right.

Joanna forced herself not to watch him as he walked away. She was such a fool, she thought irritably. He had virtually insulted her before the maid came back, and just because she had almost blown her cover she'd let him get away with it. Again!

She scowled, tearing open the individual carton of cornflakes and tipping them into the bowl Pilar had provided. She had to stop being so—impressionable. For heaven's sake, she might be inexperienced but she wasn't stupid. Constantine was expecting her to play her part and she would. Whatever it cost her.

CHAPTER SEVEN

'YOU are doing what?'

Demetri scowled. 'I am taking her on a sight-seeing tour of the island.'

Olivia stared at him. 'But—how can you?' She gave an exasperated little snort. 'Do you want her to think she is welcome here?'

'No.' Demetri felt the heat of the metal at his back burning into his pelvis but he didn't move away from the Jeep. It was important that he appeared as indifferent to his sister's complaints as possible, and lounging here in the sunlight he looked—he hoped—totally at ease with the situation. 'What would you have me do with her? Take her sailing? Or perhaps enjoy a cosy morning beside the pool?'

'Why do you have to do anything with her?' demanded Olivia irritably. 'Let her entertain herself. She will soon get bored if she has to spend all her time in her room. Then perhaps she will leave.'

'I would not hold your breath,' retorted Demetri, keeping a wary eye on the open doors of the villa. 'Mrs Manning is far more intelligent than you might think.'

Olivia gave her brother a scornful look. 'You sound as if you are infatuated with the woman, too,' she declared coldly. 'Have a care, Demetri. Our father may appreciate your taking care of his—' She used a word that even he found offensive, before adding darkly, 'But he will not be happy if you decide to take advantage of his incapacity.'

'There is no question of that,' retorted Demetri harshly, stung into an involuntary oath. '*Theos*, Livvy, what do you take me for?'

'I take you for a hot-blooded man who is deliberately putting himself in the way of an unscrupulous woman,' replied Olivia heatedly. 'Demetri, you are not going to tell me that you do not find her physically attractive, at least. The woman is sex on two legs. You must have noticed.'

'I—' Demetri was incapable of an outright lie, but he was determined not to allow Olivia to have the last word. Pushing himself away from the vehicle, he swore as the hot metal burned his palm. 'You are crazy,' he said, by way of a distraction. 'Be careful, Livvy, or I shall begin to think you are jealous.'

'Jealous! Of her!' At last he had caught her on the raw, and she gazed at him with fury in her eyes. 'I am not jealous of that creature! But I do worry about the influence she may be having on our father. He is a sick man, Demetri. Who knows what he might agree to in his weak state?'

'Like what?' Demetri was impatient, not least because he was being forced to defend Joanna.

'I do not know, do I?' Olivia sighed. 'We know she is a gold-digger. Go figure.'

Demetri's jaw compressed, but before he could say anything more a woman appeared in the entrance to the villa. It was Joanna, her glorious hair swept back from her face and secured in one of those tight knots she had been wearing the first time he'd seen her. She was still wearing the linen pants and waistcoat, he noticed, but now the vest was open over a tight black tee shirt that successfully hid most of her throat and upper arms.

So much for sex on legs, he thought drily, despising the momentary disappointment he felt. Surely Olivia couldn't complain about her appearance today.

His sister had noticed his distraction, however, and she swung round irritably, biting back the exclamation that sprang to her lips. Then, after giving her brother a contemptuous look, she immediately strode away towards the villa, passing the other woman without even acknowledging her, her whole demeanour one of outraged indignation.

Demetri saw Joanna glance after her with a puzzled look on her face and, stifling his own misgivings, he strolled with contrived casualness towards her. 'Ready?' he asked, as she came down the two shallow steps towards him. He saw the floppy straw hat she was trying to conceal beside her leg. 'I see you took my advice.'

Her eyes widened, and he wondered if she realised how innocent they made her look. But of course she did, he told himself disgustedly. Livvy was right. He was in danger of becoming infatuated with her. And that was not going to happen.

'The hat,' he pointed out shortly now, and then, forcing himself to look anywhere than at her, he added, 'I thought we could take the Jeep. The terrain inland can be pretty rough.'

Joanna nodded. 'This is an ideal place for an open-topped vehicle,' she said, squashing any hope he might have had that she'd baulk at getting windswept. 'I'm looking forward to it.'

Just who was kidding who? thought Demetri, pretending not to notice the struggle she had to open the door of the vehicle. But the idea of taking her arm, of helping her into the front seat, was not an option. He was doing his father a favour, he told himself grimly. That was all. And if, in the process, he was able to learn a bit more about their relationship, then Livvy should applaud him, not bite his head off.

As he swung himself up beside Joanna a faintly sensual perfume assailed his nostrils, and he realised he might have another reason for being glad that they were not to be confined in a closed cabin. Her nearness was enough of a provocation in itself, without being assaulted by the delicate fragrance of her skin.

Spiro came out onto the steps of the villa as he was driving away and his assistant raised a laconic hand in farewell. Demetri wondered if Olivia had sent him. Perhaps she'd hoped he'd ask the other man to join them. And perhaps he should have, he acknowledged. But it was too late now.

Theapolis was one of the larger islands in a group that lay about a hundred miles off the coast of mainland Greece. Most of the islands were rocky and arid, and depended on tourism for their livelihood, but Theapolis wasn't one of them. Oh, it had its share of tourists: island-hoppers, for the most part, who came one day and left the next, with the occasional artist or hiker thrown in for good measure. But its main source of income came from its citrus orchards and olive groves that terraced the southern half of the island with wooded slopes and lush valleys.

The Kastro estate was situated at the south-western corner of the island, just a short distance from the village of Rythmos. The main port of Agios Antonis was at the other side of the island, and ferries docked there most weekdays during the summer months.

Demetri regaled Joanna with this information as they drove inland, the roads becoming increasingly rugged as they left the cultivated coastal area behind. The land was scrubby here, coarse and primitive, with only a few goats eking out a living on the inhospitable slopes. Craggy cliffs and isolated outcrops of rock marked a barren landscape, but the views more than made up for its splendid isolation. From here, it was possible to see the whole of the island spread out below them, and although Joanna was clinging to her seat as they negotiated the track up to the ruined temple she was evidently impressed.

She had taken off her hat as they drove into the hills, the cooler air moderating the heat of the sun, but now she put up a nervous hand to check the damage. She must be aware that the breeze had played havoc with her chignon, and Demetri tried not to feel pleased with the result. There was no way she could restore it without a mirror and, as if she'd realised this, too, she tugged the rest of the hairpins out of the knot and shook her head.

Her hair tumbled down about her shoulders in glorious profusion, softening her expression and making Demetri's fingers itch to bury themselves in its silky coils. The wind lifted several strands to blow them about her face, and she attempted to twist them back behind her ears without much success.

'Damn,' she said, as he brought the Jeep to a halt on the pebbly plateau beside the ruins of the temple. She grimaced and, picking up her hat, she jammed it down onto the unruly mass. 'That will have to do.'

Leave it, Demetri wanted to say, but he didn't. Instead, controlling the urge to snatch the hat away again, he switched off the engine and vaulted out of the vehicle before temptation got the better of him. Then, walking to the edge of the plateau, he stood gazing out at the view, struggling to contain emotions that were as unwelcome as they were unfamiliar.

The door opened behind him. He heard it. Heard her canvas-booted feet land on the gravelled sweep of the plateau and then the silence as she looked about her. What was she thinking? he wondered. It was a fair bet that she wasn't fighting an unwanted desire to pull him down onto the rough grass beside the ruin's walls and tear his clothes from him. Why had he ever thought that black tee shirt was a concession to modesty? *Khristo*, she wasn't even wearing a bra.

The silence went on too long. He'd expected her to say something, maybe even come and look at the view. He had the feeling she was as eager to stay away from him as he was from her, though for different reasons. Still, he had to know what she was doing, and, glancing behind him, he found that she was waiting for him to make the next move.

Expelling a breath, he turned and walked back to the Jeep, pocketing the keys before nodding towards the windswept site of the temple. 'Do you want to look around?'

Joanna shrugged. 'Why not?' she said evenly. 'Is there much to see?'

Demetri's lips twisted. 'I suppose that depends on your point of view,' he remarked drily. 'I should tell you that any valuable artefacts have been moved to an archaeological museum in Athens, as Theapolis does not have a museum of its own. But the sacrificial altar is still here. Despite the fact that the island was converted to Christianity in the second century A.D.'

Joanna looked at him. 'You know quite a lot about the island's history, don't you?' she asked.

'Is that because you have a personal interest in antiquities, like your father?'

Demetri's expression hardened. 'I am nothing like my father, Joanna,' he said tersely, brushing past her to stride over the crumbling wall that marked the boundary of the ruins. 'If you will follow me…'

He thought for a moment that she wasn't going to go with him. Looking back, he saw that her cheeks were pink, and from her appearance he guessed she was fighting the urge to tell him to go to hell. But did she have to bring his father's name into their conversation? Didn't she understand that he was only here on sufferance? That the last thing he needed was to be reminded of who—and what—she was.

After a few moments she seemed to come to a decision, however, and, wrapping the strap of the small haversack she was carrying around her wrist, she stepped over the wall. Then, throwing back her shoulders, she tramped across to where he was waiting, meeting his wary gaze with cool, appraising eyes.

'I'm here,' she said unnecessarily. 'Shall we get this fiasco over with?'

Demetri sighed. 'I am sorry if I have offended you,' he said politely, but she wasn't having that.

'No, you're not,' she said, looking past him to where the crumbling columns of what had been the sanctuary guarded the stone altar. 'Why pretend? We both know how you really feel.'

'I doubt that,' murmured Demetri, aware that she had no idea how he really felt. 'But I apologise if I have given you the wrong impression.'

Her brows arched mockingly. 'Is that possible?' she countered. But then, as if she was not entirely sure of her ground, she added, 'Did people actually live up here?'

'I do not think so.' Demetri decided to take his lead from her. 'But, naturally, the temple was erected on the highest point of the island. It emphasised the differences between gods and goddesses and the commoners like ourselves.'

'How things have changed,' remarked Joanna in a low voice, but Demetri heard her.

'Your point being?' he prompted.

'Oh—nothing.' She moved away from him, going towards the inner courtyard. 'It's amazing that anything has survived.'

'It has not exactly been overrun in recent years,' observed Demetri, going after her. Then, 'What were you implying just now?'

She shrugged, not looking at him. 'About what?'

'You know,' he insisted, resisting the temptation to put his hand on her shoulder and swing her about to face him. 'You have a problem with me calling myself a commoner?'

'Did you?' she countered. 'I didn't notice.'

Like hell!

Demetri took a deep breath. 'Not in so many words, perhaps,' he conceded flatly. 'Look, can we stop all this sparring? If I had wanted a fight, I would have gone to the gymnasium.'

Joanna shrugged again, mounting the steps and stopping to admire the remains of a moulded pediment. 'I didn't start it.'

'But you are determined to finish it, *ne*?' suggested Demetri in exasperation. '*Theos*, Joanna, let us call a truce.'

'Another one?' she enquired at once, and then, as if acknowledging his argument, 'Tell me about Athena. Who was she?'

Demetri drew a deep breath. Then, levelly, 'She was the daughter of Zeus. His favourite, I believe. She is said to have been seated at her father's right hand in the council of the gods, *etsi ki alios*.'

Joanna glanced back at him. 'Impressive.'

'Yes.' But Demetri wasn't at all sure what she was referring to. 'She is also reputed to have invented the olive, the plough and the rake, and taught men how to build ships for peace as well as war.'

Joanna frowned. 'Wasn't she a goddess of war, or something?' she asked. 'Or was that someone else?'

'No, she was that also.' Demetri spoke tolerantly. 'She apparently inherited the weapons of thunder and lightning from her father and she is said to have used them. Against him, too, on occasion.' He gave a wry smile. 'A very formidable lady.'

Joanna smiled now. 'You don't approve?'

Demetri merely shook his head, moving past her, picking his way across the uneven ground, where the remains of marble slabs and broken friezes were half hidden in the grass. He was finding himself increasingly intrigued by her candour and he didn't trust himself to exchange this teasing banter with her. Somehow she had got beneath his guard, and his attraction to her was no longer just a physical thing.

He heard her following him, heard the sound of the wind whistling round the stunted columns, and wondered how he could have been such a fool as to bring her here. Away from the villa it was fatally easy to forget her relationship with his father, fatally easy to pretend that they were just a man and a woman spending time together, enjoying each other's company.

He swore under his breath. Where the hell had that come from? He couldn't possibly get any joy out of being with her. She was his father's mistress; at best an opportunist, at worst a gold-digger. Olivia was right. He was being reckless. He should take her back, right now.

'Your sister doesn't like me, does she?'

Joanna's voice came from right behind him, and he turned to find she was squatting down, examining some words she had found carved on a slab of marble propped against a pillar.

'I—she—'

Demetri was annoyed to find her words had disconcerted him. It was as if she'd instinctively sensed what he'd been thinking, and for a moment he was at a loss for a reply.

'What does this say?' she asked, changing the subject. 'Is it ancient Greek?'

Demetri's nostrils flared, and he was tempted to say, What else? But he realised in time that it wasn't wise to provoke her. Provocation led to stimulation and stimulation led to an arousal he didn't want to feel. So, instead of making some slick remark, he squatted down beside her to read the inscription on the plaque. His education had given him some knowledge of classical languages and, without emotion, he said. 'It is a dedication to Athena. It was probably part of the pediment that formed the portico of the temple.' He studied it for a moment, before adding, 'It extols the virtues of the virgin mother goddess.'

Joanna's head swung round to face him. 'The *virgin* mother goddess?' she echoed disbelievingly. 'Isn't—isn't that a contradiction in terms?'

Demetri found himself gazing into wide blue eyes, dark lashes—probably mascaraed, he chided himself scornfully—casting delicate shadows on her cheeks. Cheeks whose colour deepened to a rich crimson as he stared at her.

She was obviously as startled by his nearness as he was by hers, and before he could think of a satisfactory answer to her question she attempted to get to her feet. But she had acted without taking the unevenness of the ground into consideration and would have stumbled had he not lunged forward and grabbed her arm.

His action unbalanced him, however. With a feeling of helplessness he felt himself falling, and moments later he found himself on a rough bed of gravel with Joanna on top of him.

He didn't know which of them was the most dismayed by what had happened. Judging by the horrified look on Joanna's face as she endeavoured to struggle off him, she had to be in the running. But, hell, he was shocked, too. His spine had taken quite a beating, and it irritated him enormously that she probably thought he was to blame for the whole incident.

Which wasn't true, he thought frustratedly. It wasn't his fault that she hadn't taken care where she put her feet. The outraged expression she was wearing only increased his aggravation, and he couldn't understand why she was looking so annoyed.

'Will you let go of me?' she snapped, and it was only then that he realised he was still gripping her forearm. During the fall he must have held on to her, and now she was behaving as if it was all his fault.

'I did not instigate this, you know!' he exclaimed, feeling a particularly sharp stone digging into his hip. 'I was trying to save you from falling flat on your face.'

'Really?' Patently, she didn't believe him. 'Well, why don't you let me go and we'll say no more about it?'

Demetri's lips parted. Her insolence infuriated him. She was behaving as if he had engineered the whole thing. What did she expect him to get out of it, for God's sake? What pleasure did she think he got from acting as a cushion for her not inconsiderable weight?

The answer came as a treacherous stirring in his groin. Beneath her flailing arms and legs, his unwanted arousal hardened to a throbbing shaft. Thick and muscular, it thrust against the thin confinement of his shorts, an unmistakable stiffness against the softness of her stomach.

He knew the moment she felt it, too. Like a rabbit caught in the glare of headlights, she froze to an unmoving stillness, her eyes wider yet filled with a revulsion he neither knew nor understood. *Theos*, she wasn't a child. She knew something like this could happen. What did she expect when he could feel the pebble-hard pressure of her nipples against his chest?

The most sensible thing would be to push her away from him, to let her get up and hope against hope she didn't tell his father what he had done. He was fairly sure that Constantine, not to mention Olivia, would find his explanation somehow lacking in conviction, but the quicker he dealt with the situation, the less damning it would be.

Yet the panic he could see in her eyes was getting to him. Dammit, he wasn't a monster, he thought angrily. He was just a man—an attractive man, if what most women told him was true—and not someone of whom she need be afraid. He knew that somehow, some way, he had to convince her—convince himself!—that he was not to blame for what had happened. And, ignoring both her resistance and his own misgivings, he raised his arm and ran the back of his hand down her cheek.

Her skin was hot; so hot. Even the casual brush of his fingers left a livid whiteness on her flesh. A whiteness that was soon overtaken again by the heated blush that was so unexpected. But her skin was soft; so soft. It was like the smoothest satin he'd ever touched.

She didn't move. She seemed incapable of doing so now, or perhaps she was afraid of what else her unguarded actions might provoke. His arousal hadn't subsided; on the contrary, it felt as if it had increased. His whole body ached for fulfilment, his erection pulsing heavily against her hip.

Theos, he had never wanted a woman as much as he wanted her, he realised incredulously. The vision he had had earlier, of pulling her down to the ground and tearing the clothes from her, was still with him. But now it had been reinforced with an urgent desire to make love to her. To bury himself inside her and teach her how desirable it could be.

But he wanted her to want him, too. The thought of her wrapping those long, long legs about his hips, arching up beneath him, of him spilling his seed in her tight sheath, was enough to drive him almost to the edge. And why? Because he wanted to show his father what a faithless bitch she was? Or because he wanted to prove to himself that she couldn't prefer the older man?

That suspicion sickened him. What was he doing, for pity's sake? How could he even think of making love with Joanna Manning and profess to love his father as a son should? It was unforgivable. He was unforgivable. He should have taken Olivia's advice and avoided any chance of something like this happening. Olivia had been right. He was a hot-blooded man, and Joanna was just as unscrupulous as Olivia had said.

Or was she?

He stared up at her and then, hardly knowing what he was doing, he gripped her face between both hands and brought that soft, luscious mouth to his. Just one kiss, he told himself, rolling onto his side and taking her with him. If she kissed him back he'd know he'd been right all along. With her flat on the grass at his side he felt infinitely more in control of the situation, and, just for good measure, he traced the curve of her lips with his tongue.

Theos! His breath caught in his throat and, almost involuntarily, he deepened the kiss. Her lips parted and his tongue dipped irresistibly between her teeth. Heat and sweetness; warmth and wetness; she tasted as delicious as he'd anticipated. And, instead of sobering, Demetri's head swam at the first hint that she was kissing him back.

He struggled to hold onto his sanity. But when her arms rose to circle his neck he felt his control slipping away. With a little moan of submission Joanna abandoned herself to his lovemaking, surging up against him, her tongue tangling with his, her fingers curling into the hair at his nape.

It was heaven and it was hell—and it was wrong. No matter how tempting it would be to abandon his own scruples, as she had apparently abandoned hers, he told himself he couldn't do it. He had been crazy to let things get this far and he had to stop it now. With a groan of anguish, he brought his hands to her shoulders to push her away.

But his own needs betrayed him. When he touched the tight-fitting tee shirt, and realised that it was all that was between him and her breasts, good sense slid away. His fingers slipped down her arms to grip the soft curve of her midriff. With his thumbs stroking the undersides of her breasts, it took very little effort to move higher and palm the swollen peaks.

Khristo! He dragged his mouth away from hers to look at what he was doing, his breath constricting in his throat. She was so responsive, her heart palpitating wildly beneath his hands. Her chest rose and fell with the urgency of her arousal, and her scent, warm and seductive, rose to his nostrils. What was more, he thought he could happily drown in the wanton languor of her eyes.

But the look in her eyes was changing. As he watched, almost drugged by his own emotions, a look of horror returned to her face. Perhaps if he'd still been kissing her, perhaps if he'd still been plundering her mouth with the hunger he hadn't been able to deny, she wouldn't have had the chance to come to her senses. As it was, her hands at his nape became claws that tore him away from her, her flailing legs nearly unmanning him as she fought to scramble to her feet.

Before he could beat her to it, her angry tongue lashed out at him. 'How—how dare you?' she cried. 'How could you? You're—you're despicable!'

'And you are…?' suggested Demetri, in a dangerously bland tone. He got to his feet with a contrived lack of haste and regarded her with an amazingly calm look of enquiry. 'What are you, Joanna? Apart from my father's—' He broke off, knowing full well that she would finish the sen-

tence for him. 'I would like to hear your interpretation of what just happened.'

Joanna swayed. She was obviously distressed,
and he despised himself for suddenly feeling
sorry for her. She had had no shame so why
should he?

'Go—go to hell!' she said at last, somehow
summoning the strength to answer him, and, after
bending to rescue her hat, she stuffed it into her
haversack, and strode unsteadily away towards
the car.

CHAPTER EIGHT

DEMETRI left for Athens early the next morning.

Constantine gave her the news when she joined him in his suite before breakfast, and Joanna realised that Demetri must have been on board the helicopter she'd heard circling the island as she was getting dressed. She felt a shiver of relief at the knowledge that she wasn't going to have to confront him again that day, and wondered if his trip had been arranged for the same purpose.

But, no. Demetri was unlikely to let anything she did influence his actions, and Constantine's explanation—that he was going to bring his sister and her fiancé back to the island—was a bleak confirmation. He was completely without honour or conscience, and she despised herself for being a party to his betrayal of his father.

The journey back to the villa the day before had been fraught with tension. They hadn't spoken to one another after what had happened at the temple and Joanna had made a concerted effort not to look at Demetri either. She couldn't have borne to see the smug expression she'd been sure he'd be wearing, and she'd been overwhelmingly

131

relieved when the stone gateposts that guarded the entrance to the villa had loomed ahead of them. She'd leapt out of the vehicle as soon as Demetri had applied the brakes, offering him only a muffled 'Thanks' before hurrying inside.

Thanks! That had hardly been warranted, she'd chided herself later, when a maid had come to ask if she would be joining the family for lunch. Her excuse for refusing—that she had a headache and was going to rest for a while—had been just as mendacious, and she'd guessed that Demetri would see it for what it was. But she hadn't cared. She honestly didn't know how she was going to face him again, and she'd spent half the night wondering if she should tell Constantine that she couldn't continue with this charade.

But what excuse could she give? She couldn't tell Constantine what had happened, not without destroying the faith he had in his only son. Besides, the truth was her behaviour had only reinforced Demetri's opinion of her. He thought she was only using his father for her own purposes and he believed he'd proved it. But, like her, he couldn't use the argument. Not without implicating himself.

Still, Constantine did look considerably better this morning, which was a blessing. He wasn't dressed yet; when she'd joined him in his apartments he'd been resting in his chair beside his bed, wearing only his dressing gown, flicking through some of the letters and reports that Demetri had handled in his absence. Now they were sitting out on his balcony, enjoying fresh fruit and coffee and warmly scented rolls in the open air. He was still not dressed, but Joanna wasn't worried. It was so good to see him up and about again.

Buttering a roll, Joanna realised it was the first food she'd been able to face since the previous morning. The night before she'd only picked at the *mousakas* Constantine had insisted on ordering for her, and, although he had complained, she'd noticed his appetite had been sadly lacking too. Now, though, he seemed to be enjoying the peach she had peeled for him, laughing a little ruefully as the juice from the fruit insisted on dribbling down his chin.

'Um—when will—Demetri be back?' she asked at last, finishing the roll and reaching for her coffee. She had to know. She had to prepare herself for their eventual confrontation, whenever that would be.

'Ah...' Constantine wiped his mouth with his napkin and set it aside. 'Probably tomorrow,' he replied thoughtfully. 'The wedding is in less than a week, as you know. Alex will want to spend some time in her own home before Costas spirits her away to Penang.'

Joanna took a breath, trying not to think about how short-lived her respite was going to be. 'Penang?' she said, as if she'd never heard of it before. 'Is that where they're going for their honeymoon?'

'Indeed.' Constantine smiled. 'You have never been to Malaysia, Joanna?'

'No.' In fact, she had been hardly anywhere. Except Sardinia, she reminded herself bitterly. She would never forget Sardinia. 'Is it nice?'

Constantine covered her hand with his. 'It is beautiful,' he told her gently. 'Very beautiful.' He paused. 'Like you, *agapi mou*.' He paused again, and then said perceptively, 'What is wrong?'

'Wrong?' Joanna hoped he would attribute the slight tremor she could detect in her voice to astonishment. 'What could be wrong, Constantine? I am here, in one of the most perfect places in the world, with probably the kindest man I could ever hope to meet. What could I possibly find wrong with that?'

'*Veveus.*' Indeed. But Constantine was still regarding her with concerned eyes. 'So, tell me more about your outing with Demetri. Last evening you seemed a little tired, and I did not press it. Oh, you said you had enjoyed the visit to the

Temple of Athena, but you said little about Demetri himself. Was he polite to you? Did he conduct himself in a way I would have approved of?'

If the situation hadn't been so serious Joanna thought she might have laughed out loud. But it would have been a hysterical laugh, and at herself, not at his words. Dear God, how was she supposed to answer him? What was that expression about being economical with the truth?

'Demetri isn't entirely happy with—with our relationship,' she said carefully. 'But you know that.'

Constantine's mouth tightened. 'You are saying he was rude to you?'

Rude? Once again the urge to laugh was almost irresistible, but she fought it back. 'Um—not rude, no,' she managed weakly. Then, hoping to change the subject, 'He—he's very knowledgeable about the island, isn't he? I was especially interested in the stories about Athena and what she is supposed to have done—'

'Arketa!' Enough! With an abrupt cutting gesture of his hand Constantine silenced her, his lined face dark with anger. 'I am not interested in what my son had to say about our myths and legends, Joanna. I want to know what he had to say about me—about *us*.'

Joanna's lips parted in alarm. In her haste to reassure him she had obviously said the wrong thing, and somehow she had to convince him that nothing untoward had happened.

'He—didn't say anything about—about you, Constantine,' she protested urgently. 'I—I just get the feeling he doesn't like me. He thinks I'm a gold-digger. That's all I meant.'

'In other words, Demetri does not consider his father is still capable of attracting a beautiful woman,' retorted Constantine shortly. 'In his eyes I am just a pathetic old man, trying to boost his ego in the company of a trophy mistress!'

'No...' Joanna realised she had only worsened the situation, and she wished she had had more warning of what was to come. But then, she hadn't taken Constantine's insecurities into consideration. 'It's me he despises, not you.'

'Those were his words, were they?'

'No.' Joanna was floundering now. 'That's not what I meant.'

'What did you mean, Joanna?' Constantine looked weary now. '*Then pirazi*, so long as he does not suspect the truth I suppose that is all that matters, *ne*?'

'Yes.' Joanna breathed a little more freely. 'And I can assure you, he believes every word you say.'

'Good.'

Joanna hesitated. 'You're not upset, are you, Constantine?'

'Upset?' His hand fell away to his lap, and to her relief a rueful smile touched his lips. 'I suppose my ego has suffered a blow,' he admitted drily. 'But, no. I am not upset with you, my dear. I am just sorry that you had to bear the brunt of my son's displeasure. Demetri's tongue can be very—wounding. I know.'

Joanna looked down at her coffee. She didn't want to think about Demetri's tongue at that moment. Didn't want to remember what he had done with that tongue, or how warm and hungry it had felt in her mouth. He'd used his tongue to captivate her, to give her an indication of how easy it would have been for him to seduce her. And she'd let him. She'd actually encouraged him. And, whether his lovemaking had been hot and spontaneous or cold and calculating, she'd surrendered any right to judge him.

Oh, Lord...

'You would tell me if there was anything else?'

To her dismay, Constantine was still watching her and he had interpreted her expression in an entirely different way. 'Of course,' she replied hurriedly, thanking the saints that he couldn't read her mind at that moment. She picked up her cup in both hands to avoid any chance of spilling her coffee. 'Um—tell me about Alex's fiancé. Is he handsome? Has she known him long?'

Constantine heaved a sigh. 'Long enough,' he said, and she thought at first he was still preoccupied with Demetri's behaviour. But then he added, 'Costas is the son of Andrea Karadinos. Andrea is a friend as well as a business associate. Our children have known one another since they were young. It is fortunate that they appear to love one another. But Alex knows she is cementing our relationship by marrying Costas.'

Joanna stared at him. 'So it's an arranged marriage?' She didn't know why she should feel so surprised.

'In a way.' Constantine's lips twisted. 'Ah, Joanna, I can see that that troubles you.'

'No.' But it did.

And he knew it. 'You have to understand,' he said. 'Alex is my daughter. As such, she is a target for every fortune-hunter she meets. That is not to say that if she had fallen in love with a man I did not know I would necessarily have prevented her from marrying him. I am not so cruel. But it is much easier that she has chosen a man I like. I was happy to give my permission. *Etsi, kanena provlima*! No problem, *ne*?'

Joanna shook her head. 'I didn't realise you were so—so—traditional.'

'Do you not mean conventional?' enquired Constantine drily. 'I have to admit, I do have certain expectations as far as my children are concerned. Olivia went against my wishes and divorced the man I had chosen for her, and you can see how aimless her life has become. I do not want that to happen to Alex.'

'And Demetri?'

Joanna could have bitten out her tongue. Why had she asked that? After trying so hard to put thoughts of Demetri behind her, she'd said exactly the wrong thing.

Constantine was frowning now. 'Demetri?' he echoed. 'Did he mention a *filenatha* to you?'

'I—no.' Joanna was flustered again. She had heard that word before. It meant girlfriend. 'I just wondered...' ...*what you had in store for him*, she finished silently. She didn't want to acknowledge that the idea of Demetri marrying a woman of his father's choosing was a disturbing thought.

'My son knows his duty,' Constantine replied at last—which could have meant anything. 'He knows what I expect of him. He will not let me down.'

By getting involved with a woman he believes is sleeping with his father, Joanna added under her breath, still not knowing why that should matter to her.

She forced a smile. 'I'm sure you're right,' she said, assuming a lightness she didn't feel. 'Now, what shall we do this morning?'

In the event, Joanna did very little.

Constantine insisted on examining his mail before joining her on the patio downstairs, and after about half an hour he sent a message with Philip, asking that she forgive him if he didn't join her until later. There were business matters to be dealt with, Philip explained stiffly. Phone calls to be made. A backlog of decisions to be sanctioned.

The arrival of Nikolas Poros a little while later was another diversion, and signalled the death knell of any hopes she might have had of them spending the morning together.

In consequence, Joanna went back to her room, changed into her swimsuit and a wraparound skirt, and returned to the patio. She'd brought a magazine with her and, taking up a position on one of the cushioned loungers beside the pool, she tilted her face to the sun.

She'd been sitting there for perhaps fifteen minutes when she heard footsteps crossing the terrace. Olivia, she thought depressingly, wondering how she could have been so stupid as to think that Constantine's daughter would miss a chance like this. But she was pleasantly surprised when a male voice said, 'I would advise you to wear suncream, Mrs Manning. It would be unwise to risk burning such delicate skin.'

Spiro. Joanna turned her head to find Demetri's personal assistant standing beside her chair, his expression one of good humour mixed with mild concern. He was dressed in khaki shorts and a short-sleeved cotton shirt worn outside his trousers, his dark hair still damp—from his shower, she suspected.

'I did put some cream on my arms and legs before leaving my room, Mr Stavros,' she replied now, shading her eyes to look up at him. 'But thanks for the advice.'

'My pleasure,' he said smoothly, his smile revealing a row of even white teeth. 'And, please: call me Spiro.'

'All right. Spiro.' She smiled, realising that most women would find him very attractive. 'And I'm Joanna. I'm not used to answering to Mrs Manning.'

'Why?' He hooked the adjoining lounger with his foot and seated himself on the end of it. 'Is it not your name?'

Joanna's mouth drew in. 'If you're asking whether I've been married or not, then, yes. It's my name. It's just—well, most people call me Joanna.'

Spiro shrugged. 'I was curious, that is all.'

'You were? Or was it Demetri?' she countered, realising that she should not be deceived into thinking that Spiro was any more likely to want her here than his employer. 'Did he ask you to speak to me?'

'Demetri has gone to Athens.'

'To bring his sister home. I know,' said Joanna tersely, without pointing out that that wasn't what she'd asked him. 'Why aren't you with him?'

'We are not—how do you say it?—joined at the hip, *ne*?' remarked Spiro drily. 'I am his assistant, not his bodyguard.'

'His bodyguard?' Joanna caught her breath. 'Does he need one?'

Spiro studied her expression for a moment and then glanced away towards the pool. 'Perhaps,' he said. 'Sometimes.' He drew a breath. 'It is a beautiful morning, is it not?'

'Beautiful,' agreed Joanna a little dazedly, remembering what Constantine had said about security when she'd first arrived. She'd forgotten what a dangerous place the world could be, and had taken the men who surrounded Constantine for granted. He'd always dismissed them as nurses or chauffeurs, but now she realised she'd been naïve in not seeing them as bodyguards, too. This was a very wealthy family, after all. They were bound to have enemies. *Demetri* was bound to have enemies. Oh, God, why hadn't she thought of that before?

Aware that her palms were sweating, she quickly swung her feet off the lounger and sat up. The idea of Demetri needing a bodyguard had ruined her mood. She was antsy; anxiety tugged at her solar plexus. At least Constantine wasn't here to witness it, but she didn't trust Spiro not to see that she was spooked.

'I—think I'll have a swim,' she said, even though until that moment she'd had no thought of going into the water. She rubbed her arms as if they were burning. 'As you say, it is very hot.'

'He will be back tomorrow, Joanna,' Spiro remarked, getting to his feet with her and reminding her briefly of Demetri, with his superior height and muscled frame. 'He does not take chances.'

'And why should that be of any interest to me?' she asked, stepping towards the edge of the pool, then glancing back at him. 'I'll remember what you said about the sunscreen,' she added. 'Have a nice day.'

CHAPTER NINE

IN FACT Demetri didn't return to Theapolis the next day. It was two days later when the helicopter landed at the small airfield near Agios Antonis, and he couldn't deny he was glad to be back.

To make sure that Joanna hadn't caused his father any grief in his absence, he defended himself irritably. Even though he'd had Spiro's nightly reports to reassure him, he needed to see for himself. Spiro was not family, after all. How could he know what Constantine was thinking, what he was feeling? How could Spiro know what went on behind his father's bedroom door?

How could he?

Scowling, Demetri hauled off his own suit carrier and waited with some impatience for his sister and her fiancé to debark from the aircraft. *Theos*, he swore to himself, how many suitcases did they have? They were going on honeymoon for three weeks, not three months.

It was because of Alex that he'd had to delay his return to the island. She'd insisted that she'd been unable to find exactly the right headdress to wear with her wedding veil. Consequently one had had to be made for her, but it hadn't been ready until the following day.

In Demetri's opinion one headdress looked much like another, but he'd been obliged to humour her in this. It was Alex's big day, after all. If Costas was prepared to indulge her, how could he do anything less?

Costas's mother and father, and his three sisters, who were to be Alex's attendants, would be arriving the next day. And the day after that—the day before the ceremony—many more relatives and friends would be taking up temporary residence at the villa. Demetri wondered how Joanna would cope with so many strangers in the house, and then chided himself for caring what she thought about anything. She shouldn't be here; she didn't belong here. And he sure as hell shouldn't be suffering withdrawal symptoms just because he hadn't seen her for more than forty-eight hours.

The villa was ominously quiet when they arrived there in the late afternoon. Spiro had despatched the car to pick them up, but even he was absent when Demetri walked into the reception hall. Somewhere a bee was buzzing, probably trapped against the glass of the arching atrium, and the sultry scent of lilies and roses and other more exotic blossoms was strong on the air.

With a feeling of disquiet Demetri left Alex and Costas to offload their luggage and vaulted up the stairs to the first floor. The absence of servants wasn't a cause for concern. Most of the staff were free between the hours of three and six. He strode along the corridor to his father's apartments, assuring himself that he was overreacting.

He hesitated at the door. Once he would have walked in without knocking, but recent events had made him more cautious. Clenching his teeth, he raised his hand and tapped on the panels, feeling a mingled sense of relief and aggravation when Philip opened the door.

'Kirie Demetri,' the old man exclaimed warmly, in their own language. 'You are back at last. Thanks be to God!'

'Why?' Demetri brushed past the old manservant and glanced quickly about him. 'What has happened? Is my father all right?'

Philip wrung his hands. 'I wish I knew,' he said, setting all Demetri's nerves on red alert. 'I have been so worried.'

'Worried?' Demetri was sure Spiro would have told him if his father had had a turn for the worse. Or perhaps not. 'What do you mean?'

'Oh, Kirie Demetri!' Philip shook his head. 'That woman—she is no good for him.'

The fact that Demetri agreed with him made it harder for him to say tersely, 'I am sure my father knows what he is doing, Philip.' He saw his father's bedroom door was closed and took a deep breath. 'Is he resting? I would like to have a word with him—'

'He is not resting.' Philip licked his dry lips. 'They are out, *kirie*. In the heat of the day they went out. I could not stop them.'

Demetri wondered why he felt so deflated. *Na pari i oryi.* He ought to be glad his father was feeling well enough to go out. He had obviously recovered from the setback he'd been suffering when Demetri left for Athens, and it was a short step from there to presuming that, far from being no good for him, Joanna had had a favourable effect. Philip was jealous, that was all. And Demetri—well, he preferred not to dwell on his own feelings in the matter. Far better to go back downstairs and find Spiro, and try to submerge himself in the only part of his father's affairs that should concern him: the Kastro empire.

It wasn't until dinner that evening that Demetri encountered Joanna again.

He wasn't absolutely sure what time she and his father had returned from their outing—Spiro, who had been answering a call from one of their clients when Demetri and his sister had got back, had been annoyingly vague about their whereabouts. He thought they might have driven into Agios Antonis to do some shopping, but he couldn't be sure. As he'd said, Constantine hadn't consulted him before leaving the villa.

In consequence Demetri had had to cool his heels until the evening. He hadn't tried to see his father again before dinner. He was too aware of what he might find if he did. Besides, Spiro had business matters to discuss with him, and until his father was fully recovered—or he allowed Olivia to assist her brother, as she wanted to do—it was Demetri's responsibility to see that there were no foul-ups in the operating process.

His first thought, when he walked into the salon that evening and found Joanna and his father seated on a sofa, laughing together over a book Constantine had open on his lap, was that she looked even more beautiful than he remembered. In his absence the sun had given a golden glow to her fair skin and added lighter streaks to the pale glory of her hair. She was wearing a thin wraparound gown in shades of dark blue and turquoise that left one shoulder bare and clung to the lissom contours of her shapely body. A soft chignon allowed shining strands of hair to curl about her jawline, drawing his unwilling attention to the high cheekbones and the pure line of her throat. In short, she looked delectable, and Demetri knew an unforgivable urge to stride across the room and drag her away from the possessive arm his father had placed about her waist.

'Ah, Demetri.' Constantine greeted him pleasantly, and, despite his misgivings, Demetri was obliged to cross the room and bend to accept the customary salutation. But he drew the line at giving Joanna any kind of welcome, and permitted himself merely a tight smile in her direction.

He saw, to his satisfaction, that she was looking less confident now. Her lids dropped, and she made a play of being absorbed in the book. He realised now that it was a photograph album. *Theos*, he thought furiously, his father was showing her pictures of himself, Olivia and Alex when they were children. Did he have no shame?

'You will forgive me if I do not get up,' Constantine continued, shifting into a more comfortable position on the sofa. 'We have had rather a busy day, eh, Joanna? And I confess I am a little tired.'

'Busy, yes,' murmured Joanna, her eyes flickering briefly to Demetri's taut face. Then, because

Constantine obviously expected more of her, 'We—er—we've been visiting a friend of your father's.'

'Marcos Thexia,' put in Constantine smugly, mentioning the name of his lawyer. 'And we did a little shopping, too.' He lifted Joanna's wrist to display the diamond-studded bracelet that encircled it. 'What do you think, Demetri? Is it as beautiful as its wearer, do you think?'

'Constantine!'

Joanna's protest sounded convincing, but Demetri was not deluded by her tone. 'Not nearly,' he said gallantly, but the fleeting look she gave him revealed that she wasn't deceived by his insincerity either. Nevertheless, Demetri was more concerned with why his father should have been visiting his lawyer. In God's name, what had he done now?

'That is what I thought,' said Constantine happily, apparently immune to any undercurrents between them. 'Ah, here is Uncle Panos. *Pos ineh simera to vrathi, Panos*?' How are you this evening?

The old man's intervention allowed Demetri to withdraw to the other side of the room. Finding a tray of drinks on a half-moon-shaped table, he poured himself a generous measure of Scotch before turning back to face the others. He didn't know what he'd expected exactly. Perhaps that the unwelcome emotions Joanna had inspired in him before he went away had been exaggerated in his own mind. He'd assured himself that she couldn't be half as desirable as he remembered, but he'd been wrong. She was just as desirable, just as—

But his mind baulked at the ugly word that had entered his head. He didn't just want to have sex with her; he wanted to make love to her. Using her to assuage his frustrations wouldn't come close to how he was feeling. If it wasn't so bloody ludicrous he'd have wondered if he didn't want to have a relationship with her himself.

'Will you put the album away, *agapi mou*?'

As Panos seated himself in the chair closest to him Constantine asked Joanna if she'd return the photograph album to the cabinet. Then, as the two older men fell into conversation about the political situation in Athens, Joanna got to her feet and, with obvious reluctance, came towards Demetri.

Of course, he thought, with grim satisfaction. The cabinet was right next to where he was standing. To reach it she was obliged to run the gamut of his narrow-eyed appraisal, and it irritated him no end that she appeared so composed when he felt so tense and on edge.

'Did you enjoy looking at pictures of my father's offspring?' he enquired in a low voice, unable to help himself. 'Some of them must have been taken before you were even born.'

Joanna bent to slide the album back into place and his eyes were irresistibly drawn to her cleavage. Then she straightened to face him. 'You flatter me,' she said, and for a moment his mind went blank. But she enlightened him. 'I'm not as young as you apparently imagine.'

'Oh. Right.' Demetri struggled to collect his thoughts. 'Well, perhaps you have some photographs of your own family to show us, *ne*? Your husband, *isos*?' He paused. 'If there ever was such a person.'

'There was.' She spoke in a low voice. 'I wouldn't lie about something like that.'

'No?' He paused. 'But that begs the question of what you *would* lie about, *okhi*? Perhaps you have lied about something else.'

'No.' She was indignant. 'Why should you think I would have anything to hide?'

Demetri shrugged. 'I suppose because I only know what you have chosen to tell me. This sad story about your parents being killed when you were a child and having to be brought up by your aunt: do you not think it smacks a little of a fairy story, *ne*?'

She stared at him with wide, accusing eyes. 'It was no fairy story, Mr Kastro,' she told him coldly. 'My parents were killed in an avalanche in Austria and I was brought up by my father's elderly aunt. Believe me, I wouldn't make that story up.'

Demetri's brows drew together. 'You sound very sure.'

'I am.'

'Do I take it that it was not a happy time for you?'

'A happy time for me?' Joanna's face contorted. 'Mr Kastro, my whole life has not been a—a happy time for me. Does that answer your question?'

Demetri frowned. 'And with your husband?'

'My ex-husband?' Joanna clasped her hands together at her waist and stared down at them. 'Then most of all,' she added bitterly.

'What are you saying to Joanna, Demetri?'

Constantine's querulous voice broke into their exchange, and Demetri suppressed an oath when Joanna turned her head to meet his father's gaze. Immediately she seemed to realise she'd been less than discreet in discussing her personal affairs with him, and without another word she hurried back to Constantine's side.

'We were just chatting about my childhood,' she said, letting Demetri off the hook even as she proved she was as capable of bending the truth as anyone else. 'Is it nearly time for dinner?'

'When Alex and Costas get here,' agreed Constantine drily. 'Ah, here they are at last.' With her help he got heavily to his feet. 'My dear, allow me to introduce you to my younger daughter and her fiancé. Alex, Costas—this is my very dear friend, Joanna Manning.'

Dinner went reasonably well. Perhaps it was because Olivia was absent for once, but Demetri had to admit that the atmosphere was considerably less tense than when she was present.

Alex was much different from her sister, of course, and she seemed to see nothing wrong in the fact that their father should be choosing to have an affair with a much younger woman. Indeed, in an aside to her brother she observed that Constantine looked quite well for a man who only weeks ago had undergone a serious operation. Her opinion was that Joanna must be doing him some good, and Demetri was forced to concede that she might be right.

Not that that was any consolation to him. It didn't please him to realise that he was beginning to find excuses for Joanna's involvement with his father. Listening to her talk about herself, about her marriage, he'd actually felt some compassion for her. So much so that he'd resented his father for interrupting them when she'd been on the verge of telling him why her marriage had broken down. Or rather, he thought she had, he reflected wryly. Perhaps she hadn't intended to confide in him at all. Perhaps everything she'd said had been a carefully orchestrated attempt to gain his sympathy. If so, she'd certainly achieved her aim.

He scowled. Dammit, when was he going to stop thinking with his emotions instead of his head? It didn't matter if she'd lied to him or not. She wasn't his concern.

But she was.

'Is something wrong, Demetri?'

Alex's low voice, speaking in their own language, was troubled, and he realised that although she was sitting beside him he'd hardly spoken a word to her throughout the meal. Which was unusual for him. He'd always felt he had more in common with his younger sister than with Olivia. The fact that Alex was getting married in a couple of days should have been the foremost thing on his mind.

'Nothing,' he denied now, forcing a teasing smile for her benefit. 'So…how do you think it will feel to be Kyria Karadinos?'

'Pretty good, I hope.' She answered him in the same light vein. Then, more seriously, 'How about you? Not having second thoughts about your break-up with Athenee, are you?'

Demetri's smile deepened. 'No,' he said drily, aware that only Alex would have dared to bring up his affair with Athenee Sama at the dinner table. Indeed, most people avoided talking about Athenee at all—believing, quite rightly, that it was a sore subject with him.

Or it had been. He realised with a jolt of amazement that since his father had introduced him to Joanna he hadn't even thought about Athenee. Now he was, but he felt nothing. Nothing at all.

'I am glad.' Alex was nothing if not persistent. 'I never liked her. She was always so vain, so full of her own importance. She would not have made you happy, Demetri. You need someone warm; someone—sympathetic.' She dimpled, her face— with its straight nose and deep-set dark eyes—so like his own. 'Someone like Joanna,' she added mischievously. 'What a pity Papa saw her first.'

Demetri managed to retain his smile, but only just. As always, Alex had rushed in where angels feared to tread. 'I do not think Mrs Manning likes me,' he said, with what he thought was admirable restraint. He took a deep breath and changed the subject. 'Costas.' He leaned past her to speak to her fiancé. 'I hope you intend to keep my sister in order. I regret she has the unforgivable tendency of poking her nose into places where it is least wanted.'

'Well, I had to be sure that you were not pining for Athenee,' protested Alex indignantly. 'I am sure you know that Papa has invited Aristotle Sama to the wedding, and it is not beyond the realms of possibility that Athenee will come with him.'

Demetri's scowl returned. 'And Benaki?' he enquired, with rather less sanguinity.

'Oh, did you not know?' Alex gave a nervous little shrug of her shoulders. 'Athenee and Peri Benaki are no longer an item. Sara, Costas's sister, told me.'

CHAPTER TEN

IT WAS early evening before Joanna had the chance to escape from the wedding party. Avoiding the marquee, where earlier in the day a sumptuous lunch had been served to over a hundred guests, she went down the steps towards the beach, taking off her heeled sandals when the sand started to ooze between the straps.

From Alex and Costas's point of view it had been a successful day. Although Alex had confided that the guest list had had to be pruned because of her father's illness, Joanna couldn't help thinking that getting on to one hundred and fifty witnesses was fairly generous by anyone's standards. Another ceremony was already being planned, to take place in Athens when the young couple returned from their honeymoon, to include all the people they had not been able to invite to the island. But for the present the celebrations were over; Alex and her new husband had left for Malaysia, and all that was left to do was bid goodbye to the guests who had stayed at the villa.

Half an hour ago Joanna had escorted Constantine to his apartments, aware that he had been exhausted by it all. Despite his grim determination to give Alex a day she would remember, at the end he had had to admit his weaknesses. Without Joanna's help he would never have got up the stairs, but he was adamant that no one else should be involved.

Demetri had been concerned, of course. Joanna had been aware of him keeping an eye on his father, like herself, during the service, ready to rush to his aid if he'd looked in danger of imminent collapse.

But Constantine had drawn on strengths even Joanna hadn't believed he possessed. He'd escorted his daughter to the ceremony, stood by while she'd taken her vows, and given his speech at the lunch that followed with every indication that he was enjoying the occasion just as much as everybody else.

And he had. He'd kept Joanna at his side, of course, despite the many disapproving looks from his older daughter. It was the only intimation Joanna had had that perhaps he didn't feel as confident of his stamina as he pretended. But, apart from that, he'd behaved like any other father, proud of his daughter and eager to demonstrate his approval of her choice of husband to the world.

Thankfully, it was all over now. Joanna could feel her own tension easing as she trod across the still warm sand. Constantine had achieved his objective, and there'd been no doubt of his gratitude towards her as she'd helped him out of his jacket and shirt and replaced them with a silk dressing robe.

Subsiding with evident relief onto his bed, he'd clung to her hand for a moment longer than was necessary, saying weakly, 'You do not think anyone suspected, do you, *agapi mou*?' and Joanna had assured him that he'd done as he'd intended.

'Alex suspected nothing,' she'd assured him. 'Demetri...' She'd hesitated. 'Demetri was concerned that you might be over-taxing your strength, but none of them guessed the truth. However...' She paused again. 'You've got to tell them now, Constantine. It's only fair.'

Constantine's nod of understanding had hardly been a promise, but Joanna had had to be content with it. The old man had already been drifting into unconsciousness, and she'd left his room feeling that she'd done all she could for the present.

She took a deep breath of the salt-laden air. It had been a good day, she told herself determinedly. Constantine had enjoyed it; everyone had enjoyed it. Even she'd felt a twinge of emotion when Alex had appeared, slim and enchanting in the wedding gown that a famous designer had made especially for her. She'd been forced to admit that not everybody's wedding day was doomed to end in disappointment and humiliation. Costas loved Alex; anyone could see that. And she had only to look at them to know that the intimacy they shared was real, not imagined.

It had all been so different from her own wedding day. Oh, she had been just as eager, just as excited, but she hadn't had any idea that the day would end in the way it had. She'd never dreamt that the reason Richard had refrained from making love to her before their marriage was because he couldn't; that the man she'd thought was his friend was in fact his lover.

If only Richard could have been honest with her; honest with his parents. Goodness knew, being homosexual was not something to be ashamed of. Why couldn't he have faced his real identity instead of involving her? Was it only, as he'd said, because she'd been so trusting? Or rather because she'd been so incredibly easy to deceive?

She felt a lump come into her throat at the memory. She *had* been trusting, and naïve. Aunt Ruth had seen to that. She'd treated her niece like a servant. No wonder Joanna had been so eager to escape to a better life.

The holiday in Sardinia had been her first chance to act like a real woman. An attractive woman, moreover. One capable of appealing to a sophisticated man like Richard. Meeting him had seemed like a dream come true. He'd been so charming; so handsome. So kind that she'd fallen headlong in love with him almost on their first date.

Of course she hadn't been looking for his faults. And in the beginning she'd felt only gratitude when he'd expected so little from her. She'd had no experience with men. No experience at all except the admiration of boys when she'd been at school. The prospect of getting married had been a big step for her. It had been enough to be going on with.

Richard's parents had been kind to her, too. A much older couple than her own parents would have been, they'd virtually given up all hope of having a child of their own when Richard was born.

Naturally, they doted on him. Nothing was too good for him. He could do no wrong. Afterwards Joanna had had to acknowledge that his parents were partly to blame for what had happened. They'd expected so much of him. If they'd been younger, more worldly-wise, Richard might have found the courage to tell them the truth.

Perhaps they had suspected, Joanna reflected now. But if so they had never voiced their suspicions to her. They'd let her go ahead with the wedding, insisting on paying for everything in spite of her protests. It was the least they could do, they'd insisted, for the woman who was going to make Richard such a wonderful wife.

The day itself had gone remarkably smoothly. Richard's cousin had been best man, and much later Joanna had realised why he'd seemed so detached from the ceremony. She guessed he knew the truth and had tried to reason with Richard himself. But, for whatever misguided reasons, Richard had been determined to go through with it. Nothing was going to stop him from being the son his parents thought he was.

They'd spent the first night of their honeymoon at a hotel at Gatwick Airport. They were to spend their honeymoon in Antigua, compliments of the older Mannings, but their flight hadn't been until the next morning.

In consequence, it had been comparatively early in the evening when they'd gone to bed. Joanna had been wearing a white lace nightgown, she remembered, bought especially for the occasion. When she'd emerged from the bathroom and found Richard apparently already asleep she'd stifled her own disappointment and got obediently into bed beside him.

She hadn't gone to sleep, however. The excitement of the day and her own unsatisfied expectations had kept her awake. That had been why, when Richard had got out of bed at about half past eleven to go to the bathroom, she'd spoken to him. She'd caught his hand as he'd crept around the bed, and discovered that he wasn't at all pleased that she was awake.

She'd excused his irritation on the grounds of over-tiredness, but when he'd climbed back into bed she'd moved towards him eagerly. His pyjamas had been a little off-putting, but she'd consoled herself with the thought that he'd soon feel differently when he'd kissed her.

But Richard hadn't wanted to kiss her. To her intense humiliation he'd told her that he just wanted to go to sleep. He wasn't a physical person, he'd added, when he'd sensed her mortification. There'd be plenty of time for them to get to know one another in that way once they reached the Caribbean.

It hadn't happened. Oh, Richard had tried to make love to her on several occasions, but even Joanna, innocent as she was, had been able to see that he simply wasn't interested in her. He'd apologised, of course. Made excuses about the heat and various other irritations, which she didn't want to remember now. And still she hadn't realised what was really wrong. That her woman's body repelled him, just as another woman's body would have repelled her.

With the honeymoon over, life had returned to normal, or as near normal as possible in the circumstances. Richard had gone back to work and Joanna had managed to get a job at Bartholomew's. To all intents and purposes—certainly so far as Richard's parents had been concerned—they'd had a happy marriage.

Until Joanna had come home early from work one day and found Richard with John Powers, the young man with whom he'd been on holiday in Sardinia.

God, she thought now. How could she have been so stupid for so long? How long would she have gone on believing that Richard was simply not a physical person, as he'd said? She liked to think she'd have found out eventually, but she'd been so busy convincing herself and everyone else that he was a wonderful husband that she might well have overlooked the most obvious explanation.

With his exposure, Richard had taken another tack. She mustn't leave him, he'd insisted. He'd be devastated if she walked out on their marriage

now. And if his parents found out... The threat
had been implicit in his words. He hadn't actually
said that he would do something desperate, but
even Joanna had been able to understand how aw-
ful that would be.

So she'd stayed. For a little while, at least.
Until the day Richard had suggested she should
find herself a lover and get pregnant. It was the
only way, he'd insisted. She'd been amazed at his
insensitivity. His parents had already started asking when they were going to start a family, he'd
continued, and she wanted children, didn't she?
He'd paused then, before adding that he could
always fix her up with somebody he knew if finding a partner would be too difficult for her...

'Where is my father?'

Joanna started violently. She'd been so absorbed with the painful content of her thoughts
that she'd been unaware that she was no longer
alone. But she realised now that Demetri had
come up beside her, his tread keeping pace with
her bare feet, his suede boots already stained with
seawater.

'You're ruining your boots,' she said without
answering him. 'You should have taken them
off.'

Demetri's stare was almost palpable. 'Has he
retired for the night?' he asked harshly, ignoring

her words, and she was reminded that she had
spent the days since his return from Athens avoiding any personal contact with him. In fact, apart
from a compulsory greeting now and then, voiced
for his father's benefit, she had had no conversation with Demetri at all since their visit to the
ruined temple.

'He's having an early night, yes,' she replied
at last, not looking at him. 'Do you want me to
give him a message?'

'No. No, I do not,' he retorted shortly, and she
guessed he resented her for asking.

But why should she care? It wasn't as if it mattered what Demetri thought of her. In a few days,
a week at most, she'd be leaving the island and
she'd never see him again.

Oh, God!

Her stomach hollowed and she pressed a nervous hand to her midriff. It was what she and
Constantine had planned, she reminded herself.
What she wanted. But her stay on Theapolis had
proved far more devastating than she could have
imagined.

'How is he?'

Demetri seemed determined to pursue this conversation and Joanna expelled an unsteady breath.
She wished he would go away, back to the
women of his own nationality, many of whom

had shown their willingness to share his company. Young and old alike, all had seemed to blossom in his presence, faces flushed and excited lips parted in anticipation, ready to agree with him whatever he chose to say.

It had sickened Joanna. She hated to admit the fact that she'd noticed, but, seated at Constantine's side for most of the day, she'd found it impossible to avoid seeing that Demetri attracted women like a magnet. And she was just like them, she acknowledged bitterly. She was just as gullible. Despite her experience with Richard, she couldn't deny that Demetri had stripped away her defences and shown her she was just as vulnerable as anybody else.

And why now? she asked herself depressingly. Why after all these barren years was she attracted to a man whose only emotion was contempt? Was this her fate? Was this destiny? Was she the kind of woman who must always be a victim?

'He's tired,' she said at last, forcing herself to continue walking along the shoreline. At least her feet were cool, she thought, even if the rest of her body was burning up. 'Surely you expected that?'

'I expect nothing, Joanna,' he responded coldly. 'Then I am not disappointed.' He paused. 'How about you? Did the day live up to your expectations?'

'Like you, I have no expectations.' Joanna answered him just as coldly, convinced there was a hidden meaning behind his words. Then, because she felt too brittle to indulge in any kind of infighting with him, she added, 'Why don't you go back to your guests? I'm sure at least half of them must be suffering withdrawal symptoms by now.'

She heard his swift intake of breath. 'Jealous?'

Pain filled her. 'Yeah, right,' she managed, with just enough irony in her voice. She quickened her step to get away from him. 'Grow up, Demetri!'

He came after her. His breathing matched hers in pace, but she doubted his heart was palpitating in his chest. All the same, when he gripped her upper arm to halt her, and swung her round to face him, she was surprised by the sudden anguish in his expression.

'Oh, yes,' he said, his tone harsh and unforgiving. 'I had forgotten. You prefer your men to be older—much older. Why? Can you not—what is the word?—*hack it* with someone of your own age, *ne*?'

Joanna pressed her lips together so that he shouldn't see how his words had upset her. 'Well, there's no fear of that with you, is there, Demetri?' she countered scornfully, not caring what she said, just so long as she hurt him as he was hurting her. 'Young or old; they're all alike. They can't wait for the heir to the Kastro fortune to put his hand up their skirts!'

She had shocked him. Dear Lord, she had shocked herself. What she had said was unforgivable, and his face briefly mirrored his disbelief. Then, with an oath, he lifted his hand, and she winced in anticipation of the blow that she was sure was to come.

But he didn't hit her. Instead, his hand settled heavily on the back of her neck and, drawing her towards him, he ground his forehead against hers in a helpless gesture of what she suspected was frustration.

Yet when he spoke, his words sounded tortured. 'Why do we do this?' he demanded, his voice low and impassioned. 'I know you want me, and heaven knows I want you.'

Joanna didn't know what to say, how to answer him. She was afraid this was just another attempt to prove he was right about her, to humiliate her, to satisfy himself that she was as unprincipled as his accusations implied.

But before she could say anything a light laugh disturbed them. 'Demetri?' came a teasing voice. *'Ti tha kanateh?'*

Joanna felt Demetri's hand tighten convulsively for a moment, and then she was free. With admirable self-assurance, he'd turned to confront the woman—what else? Joanna derided herself bitterly—who had interrupted them. Speaking in his own language, he evidently gave some explanation for what he had been doing, and the woman's smile thinned only briefly before returning as confidently as before.

Joanna recognised her now. Even in the fading light it was impossible not to remember her. Her name was Athenee. Athenee Sama. Her father, Aristotle Sama, was a friend of the Kastros, and Constantine had confided to her that he and Athenee's father had had high hopes that their offspring might make a match of it.

She was certainly beautiful, thought Joanna, feeling a pang of envy. She didn't see how Demetri could fail to be attracted to her. The woman was gazing at him with such a look of admiration in her eyes that for all Demetri had said he wanted *her*, Joanna felt sure she must have misunderstood him. Beside Athenee's sweep of night-dark hair and vivid complexion, she felt pale and insignificant. A not-unfamiliar emotion for her, she conceded dully, but not one she had experienced since Constantine became her friend.

She would have escaped then. Taking several careful steps, she tried to slip away without being noticed, but Demetri had other plans. She wasn't sure whether he'd heard her—her feet had sunk into the damp sand—or he'd just remembered she was there. Whatever, his hand shot out and captured her wrist, imprisoning her beside him. Then, with casual courtesy, he asked her if she and Athenee had been introduced.

'But naturally.' It was Athenee who answered him, and the eyes she turned on Joanna weren't half as friendly. 'She is your father's—um—confidante, *ne*?' She made it sound like a dirty word. 'Constantine introduced us himself. He is, I think, very enamoured of her, is he not?'

Her meaning was obvious, and Demetri wasn't indifferent to the implication, Joanna saw at once. His hand dropped from her arm and she was left with an unwarranted feeling of isolation. And of being despised on all sides, she thought. Athenee didn't like her; that was apparent. And she had no doubt that, if he heard of it, Constantine wouldn't approve of the strangely clandestine relationship Joanna was having with his son.

'It is getting dark,' said Demetri abruptly, without answering her question. 'Come.' He included Joanna in the invitation. 'People are leaving. We should get back to the villa.'

'I'd rather stay here,' Joanna declared, determined not to lay herself open to any more insults from his girlfriend. 'You go.' Her lips twisted. 'Both of you.'

Demetri's eyes darkened. 'Joanna—'

'I'll see you in the morning,' she said, turning away. 'Goodnight.'

CHAPTER ELEVEN

IT WAS after midnight before Demetri went to his own apartments.

He told himself it was because there'd been a lot of clearing up to do after the guests who were leaving had departed, but in all honesty his father's staff were more than capable of dealing with the aftermath of the wedding party. Indeed, they'd probably seen his presence as something of an encumbrance. No doubt they'd wished he would just go away and leave them to it.

But the truth was, Demetri dreaded going to bed. So long as he was with other people he could put the turmoil of his thoughts to the back of his mind. He couldn't forget them, but he could ignore them, and that was almost as good. However, he knew that once he lay down and closed his eyes he'd have no defence against their torment.

Of course it needn't have been that way. Athenee, the woman he'd once believed he desired above all others, had shown him quite clearly that she wanted to renew their relationship. She would have been happy to stay on at the villa. Her father had had to get back to Athens; his helicopter had left earlier in the evening. But Athenee hadn't wanted to go with him. If Demetri had said the word she'd have been waiting for him now, the ideal antidote to what was wrong with him.

Yet Demetri had offered no invitation. After leaving Joanna on the beach, he and Athenee had walked back to the villa in total silence. He doubted if he'd have spoken to her at all if she hadn't caught his arm as they were crossing the terrace, and even then he'd left her in no doubt of his irritation at her interference.

'Yes?'

No warmth there, and Athenee had responded to it in her own arrogant way. 'You cannot have her, Demetri,' she'd said carelessly, and he'd known a moment's panic that his feelings were on display for all to see. But then her next words had reassured him. 'You were going to kiss her just now. I know it. But I interrupted you.' Her lips twisted. 'Be grateful to me, Demetri. Do you want your father to cut you off without a cent?'

'I do not know what you are talking about, Athenee,' he'd replied swiftly, glad of the fading light to hide the dark colour that had flooded his cheeks. 'And if this is an attempt to persuade me that you are here to console me for imagined temptations, then I regret to say that I must disappoint you.'

'Are you sure?' Athenee's eyes had flashed angrily.

'I am sure,' he'd told her. 'Nice try, Athenee, but you are wasting your time.'

'As are you, *agapitos*,' she'd retorted, determined to have the last word. 'Constantine would kill you if he ever found out.'

Would he?

Demetri posed the question to himself now, and then dismissed it. He had no intention of finding out so it didn't matter either way. But Athenee was right about one thing. He had been going to kiss Joanna, would have done so if Athenee hadn't interrupted them. He wouldn't have been able to prevent himself from tasting that sweet tempting mouth again. And how sensible was that?

Throwing off his jacket and tie, he raked frustrated fingers through his hair. Dammit, what was wrong with him? Had it been so long since he'd had a woman that he was willing to do anything, no matter how reckless, to get laid? But if that were the case why hadn't he taken up any of the invitations he'd been offered today? He wasn't a conceited man, but he knew when women were coming on to him. Yet he'd blanked them all. Including Athenee.

He scowled, and, unlatching the glass doors, stepped out onto the balcony.

It was a beautiful night. An arc of stars wheeled overhead. Although sometimes the days at this time of the year could be uncomfortably hot, the nights were infinitely more inviting. Even the insects seemed to have taken a breather and the air was overwhelmingly sensual.

Sensual.

He stifled a groan. The word reminded him of the first time he'd met Joanna. He was trying not to think about her, but just a word like that brought a stream of images pouring into his head.

It was the way she'd described the heat on Theapolis, he remembered. Sensual, she'd called it, challenging him with those deep blue eyes that seemed capable of seeing right into his soul. He'd thought she was trying to provoke him, and perhaps she had been. But he knew her better now, and he sensed that, for all her sexy clothes and striking beauty, she was not flirtatious. In fact there was something almost innocent about her at times. And there was no denying that when he'd kissed her at the temple her response had been deliciously unrehearsed.

Or perhaps he was only fooling himself, he thought irritably. He believed it would take a clever woman indeed to deceive him, but what if she was that woman? Was he being blinded by his own unwilling attraction to her? Was she using that to disguise a character that was far more complex than even he could imagine?

He didn't know. In fact, he knew precious little about her. His father seemed to have great faith in her, but what did that mean? Constantine had been ill; very ill. How did he know she hadn't used his illness to get close to him? It seemed mightily suspicious that from being some kind of clerk in an auction house she had graduated to wearing designer clothes and flaunting the friendship of a man like Constantine Kastro.

Friendship!

Demetri's stomach felt hollow. Friendship wasn't the half of it, he thought angrily, deliberately feeding his revulsion in an attempt to dispel the bitter jealousy that was gripping him. She wasn't his father's friend; she was his mistress. Did Constantine have any idea of what he was risking, getting involved with a woman like her?

Probably not, he decided grimly. And now that the wedding was over perhaps it was time he made more of an effort to find out all there was to know about Mrs Joanna Manning. Where did she live, for instance? Had she really had an un-happy childhood? And where was this elusive ex-husband who, according to her, had made her life so miserable? How long had they been married? Why had the marriage broken up? Did Constantine know? Did anybody know? Or was her past, like her present, shrouded in mystery?

He supposed he could put Spiro onto it. His assistant was a computer genius, and it would take him only a short time to discover everything Demetri wanted to know. All he needed was an address and the place she banked, and Spiro could hack into the appropriate records. In a matter of hours he'd have a file that even the secret police would be proud of.

The trouble was, that was illegal. He could hire a private detective, of course. But if his father ever found out that someone had been checking up on Joanna without his permission there'd be hell to pay. It wouldn't matter if the investigation was justified. Constantine demanded total loyalty from his employees and his family, and Demetri would bear the brunt of his father's wrath.

No, if he wanted to learn anything about Joanna he would have to do it himself. But how? How did one investigate someone about whom he knew so little? And whatever he decided to do, it had to be fairly soon.

He didn't know why, exactly, but he had the feeling that time was running out on him. He still didn't know why his father had been to see his lawyer, and the possible implications of that visit filled him with suspicion. Spiro had asked him at the beginning of the week whether he thought his father planned to marry Joanna, and he'd dismissed the idea at the time. But now it wasn't half so unimaginable as it had seemed then.

He walked to the rail that edged the balcony and stood for several minutes staring down at the gardens below his windows. Though mostly in darkness, one or two bulbs were still burning, lighting the paths and giving an eerie radiance to the shrubs that surrounded them.

The marquee was still standing on the lawns below the terrace. The contractors would be coming to take it down in the morning, but until then it stood there like a ghostly shroud. He didn't like the metaphor and turned away abruptly. It would be morning soon enough, and he had to get some sleep.

Sleep! His lips twisted. How could he sleep with the knowledge that Joanna was sleeping with his father at the other side of the house? In fact, the balcony he was standing on now wrapped right around the upper floor of the villa. He had only to turn a couple of corners and he'd be standing outside the very room where Constantine and Joanna slept.

His nerves tightened as a thought occurred to him. If Joanna was sleeping with his father, it followed that her room would be unoccupied right now. It was separated from his father's apartments by a sitting room and double panelled doors, as he knew only too well. If she'd left the window unlatched—and it was possible—he'd have an opportunity to go through her belongings without anyone being any the wiser.

He didn't know what he expected to find, though there was bound to be some identification among her papers. Her passport, for instance. He'd find her address, at least, and then it would be up to him whether he took it any further; whether he told Spiro what he'd done.

His nerves tingled as he went back into his bedroom and stripped off the white shirt he had worn for his sister's wedding. He replaced it with a short-sleeved black tee shirt that, together with his dark trousers, made him a much less conspicuous target in the moonlight.

His lips twisted. *Theos*, he wasn't used to this. No matter what justification he gave to himself, he didn't like it. It smacked too much of attempted voyeurism, and, although he wasn't planning on invading his father's bedroom and checking that they were together, if he was caught—

But he wouldn't be caught, he assured himself. As well as Joanna's sitting room, his father's sitting room lay between him and his father's bedroom. They'd never hear him. And if the window was locked it was all hypothetical anyway.

The window wasn't locked. In fact it was standing slightly ajar, and there was a lamp burning in the room. Demetri saw the light shining out onto the balcony and cursed his ill luck.

He was tempted to turn back, but something— some intuition, perhaps—urged him to go on. There was no sound and, flattening himself against the wall, he took a surreptitious glance into the room.

It was empty. The doors to his father's apartments were closed, and although the door to Joanna's bedroom was open there was no light in there. It looked as if leaving the lamp on had been an oversight. He pressed himself back against the wall again, trying to decide what to do.

This was ludicrous, he thought. She wasn't there. He was so attuned to Joanna's presence that he felt sure he'd have sensed it if she'd been in her own bed. Okay, leaving the window open had been foolish, but there had never been any real danger on the island. Constantine had probably told her that the grounds were patrolled after dark, and maybe she'd had other things on her mind when she'd left the sitting room.

He scowled. This was not the time to be thinking about what those things might be. Pull yourself together, he ordered impatiently. He didn't have a lot of time. It was already after two a.m.

Pushing the window wider, he waited only a second before easing into the room. His heart was hammering in his chest and he had to suppress a gulp of harsh laughter. *Theos*, what had she brought him to? Here he was, breaking into his own home!

Well, hardly breaking in, he amended, crossing the room on cautious feet. He frowned. But he ought to have an explanation prepared in case one of the servants disturbed him. What excuse could he give for being here? That he'd heard an intruder? Did that sound feasible? All right, his rooms were nowhere near Joanna's, but he could always say he'd been taking an evening stroll along the balcony when he'd seen someone enter this room.

He shook his head. An evening stroll at two o'clock in the morning? Who was going to believe that?

Well, it didn't matter what anyone else believed. They didn't have to believe him. He was doing this for his father, no one else. He deserved to know if the woman who had his confidence was worthy of the honour.

Yeah, right!

His deviousness appalled him. He wasn't doing this for his father; he was doing it for himself. But it wasn't sensible to be conducting an inquest on his character right now. He was here for a purpose, and the sooner he found what he was looking for, the sooner he could get back to his own room.

The sitting room offered no solutions. Apart from the sandals she'd been wearing earlier, which she'd kicked off near the balcony doors, there was nothing to show that this was Joanna's room. Any personal items must be in the bedroom and, stifling a feeling of apprehension, he moved to the bedroom doorway.

He would have to turn on a light, he realised. Although he'd regretted the lamp in the sitting room, it had made searching the place that much easier. In here, with the blinds drawn, there was no illumination whatsoever. Tiptoeing over to the bed, he listened intently for the sound of breathing, but he couldn't hear anything. Expelling a sigh of relief, he stepped back and turned on the lamp.

As he'd expected, the bed was empty. But— and this was disturbing—the sheets were tumbled and there was the definite imprint of a head on one of the lace-trimmed pillows.

His brows drew together. She must have gone to bed before his father had sent for her. The old man had returned early, after all. He'd probably been asleep when she'd come upstairs. So what, then? Had he woken up? Or was she the one who'd decided she needed his company?

That was harder to stomach. No matter how often he told himself he shouldn't be surprised by anything she did, he always was. He wanted her to be something she was not, he realised painfully. But what?

He didn't know what made him glance behind him just then. He'd observed her handbag lying on the ottoman at the foot of the bed, and he should have been moving towards it. But instead he looked round—and found Joanna herself standing in the open doorway.

He supposed he ought to be grateful that she hadn't screamed. Finding a dark-clad man in her bedroom would have been enough to spook most women, but not her. How long had she been standing there watching him? And why, when he should have been refining his story to explain this

intrusion, could he only stare at her with undis-
guised hunger in his eyes?

She looked so beautiful, he thought, his own
forbidden passion for her never more acute than
at this moment. She was wearing a silk negligee
over a matching nightgown in a particularly sub-
tle shade of gold that complemented her skin. The
cord was tied loosely at her waist and her hair
tumbled, soft and lustrous, about her shoulders.
She looked like his every dream—and his every
nightmare. He wanted her—but he couldn't have
her. She wasn't his. And that knowledge was tearing him apart.

'Demetri.' She said his name softly, with a dis-
concerting lack of surprise. 'What are you doing
here? Did Constantine send for you?'

Constantine!

The mention of his father's name brought him
briefly to his senses. 'Does he know I am here?'

She blinked. 'Don't you know?'

Demetri shook his head to clear it. 'No,' he
said in a low voice. 'That is—I did not come to
see my father. I came to see you.' He paused, but
he had to know. 'Where have you been?'

'I was with your father,' she said, her voice
barely more than a whisper. Her words crucified
him. 'Why did you want to see me? I—' She

broke off, as if just realising what time it was. 'It's the middle of the night!'

'I know what time it is,' muttered Demetri, wondering what had possessed him to tell her the truth. He should get out of here right now.

'Then—?'

He threw caution to the winds. 'We did not finish our conversation earlier.'

He saw at once that she knew what he was talking about, but he saw just as clearly that she chose not to admit it. 'What conversation would that be?' she demanded contemptuously. And then, as if realising their voices might carry on the still night air, she lowered her tone. 'I think you'd better go.'

'No.' No matter how unwise this was, he had to have some answers. 'We need to talk.'

'Without being interrupted by one of your many girlfriends?' she enquired coldly. She stepped aside from the doorway. 'Go! Go now! Before I decide to start screaming that there's an intruder in my room.'

'You would not do that.'

'No?'

'No.' He took a deep breath. 'I believe you have more—respect for my father than that.'

'But you don't,' she retorted in a low angry tone. 'Have a care, Demetri. I haven't told him about what happened at the temple yet, but that doesn't mean I won't.'

'Joanna…'

He started towards her, but she backed away into the sitting room. She was shaking her head as she groped behind her, trying to avoid falling headlong over the sofa that stood in the middle of the floor. Her hair was a pale aureole in the lamplight, accentuating the sudden colour that was spreading up her throat. She had never looked more lovely, more desirable. Or more untouchable.

Then she parted her lips, and Demetri didn't think before acting. He told himself later that he'd been afraid she was going to scream, as she'd threatened, but that wasn't the whole truth. Covering the space between them, he caught her as she would have whirled away, jerking her back against him and silencing that tempting mouth with his hand.

He didn't know which of them was the most shocked by the experience. She seemed to freeze, her whole body stiffening in outrage and disbelief. For his part, his senses were immediately assailed by the fragrance of her hair, the scent of lemon and verbena mingling with the warm perfume of her body.

But his moment of respite didn't last long. Almost at once she started to struggle against the confining circle of his arm, the muffling indignity of his hand across her mouth. She was stronger than he'd thought, and he had to fight to keep her anchored against him, his own body responding to the spicy heat she was exuding.

'Efkolos, efkolos,' he said hoarsely. Easy, easy. 'I am not going to hurt you. I just want to talk with you, that is all.'

Her response stunned him. Instead of giving up the unequal battle, she only increased her efforts to get away from him. And before he had time to assimilate his position, to decide how, if at all, he could reason with her, he felt a searing pain in his hand.

Khristo, she had bitten him!

He couldn't believe it. Letting her go now, without caring for the consequences, he gazed down at the blood oozing out of the soft flesh of his palm. He stared incredulously at the line of teeth marks that defined the bite, and then lifted his head to stare at her. She was crazy, he thought blankly. And he was crazy for thinking she would listen to him.

But she didn't scream.

Although she'd put the width of the room between them, she made no attempt to summon assistance. On the contrary, she was standing twisting her hands together at her waist, and when their eyes met he was almost sure he saw remorse in their depths.

He knew he should go. Whatever was going on here, he wasn't going to solve it by appealing to her better nature. But all the same he couldn't leave without saying incredulously, 'Why?' He lifted his hand and a drop of blood fell onto the rug at his feet. 'Why this?'

She untangled her hands and pressed one to her throat. 'You wouldn't understand.'

'Try me.'

Her tongue circled her upper lip. 'I think you ought to put a plaster on that cut.'

Demetri's mouth twisted. 'Why? Am I in danger of contracting blood poisoning, too?'

Joanna hesitated and then, incredibly, she said, 'You'd better come into the bathroom. I think I've got something you can use in there.'

Demetri's jaw dropped. 'You are offering to tend to my injury?' he asked disbelievingly, and her eyes darted away from his.

'The—the bathroom's through here,' she mumbled, instead of giving him an answer. She sidestepped past him and went through the bedroom to the bathroom beyond. A light went on and, against his better judgment, Demetri cupped his injured hand in his other palm and moved to support himself against the frame of the bedroom door.

He couldn't see into the bathroom itself, but the mirrors that lined the walls threw back the reflection of Joanna riffling through the cabinet, taking out tubes and packets of plasters, extracting cotton wool balls from what he assumed was her own toilet bag. Her industry would have amused him if he hadn't felt such a baffling sense of confusion.

Then she came to the open doorway. 'Are you coming?' she asked, still avoiding his gaze. 'I think you ought to wash it first.'

Feeling a little as if he'd stepped into some parallel universe, Demetri straightened and walked around the bed to where she was waiting. He now saw that what she was holding was antiseptic ointment and, stepping back, she indicated that he should rinse his palm at the sink.

He did as she suggested, and then acquiesced again when she gestured for him to sit on the side of the bath. Taking a swab of cotton wool, she dried his palm first and then, with evident reluctance, took his wrist between her fingers.

'This may hurt,' she said, squeezing a little of the antiseptic cream onto the wound, and he gave her a weird look.

'Tell me about it,' he remarked drily, in an effort to distract himself from the dusky cleavage she exposed when she bent over him. 'Why did you do it?'

She sighed, her warm breath fanning his palm. 'Let's just say I don't like anyone—*any man*—forcing me to—to do something.'

'Is that what you think I was doing?' protested Demetri, horrified. 'For God's sake, Joanna, I meant what I said. I would never hurt you.' Unable to help himself, he used his free hand to lift her chin so that he could look into her face. 'You believe me, do you not?'

He saw her swallow, saw the convulsive movement of her throat as she endeavoured to sustain his invasive stare. Then, with a nervous movement of her shoulders, she lifted her chin out of his hand and looked back at her task. 'You don't understand.'

'No, I do not,' he agreed huskily. 'So why do you not enlighten me?'

She took a deep breath, and after removing the surplus ointment from around the cut she smoothed a plaster over it. He thought she wasn't going to say anything more, but suddenly she lifted her head and looked at him again.

'My—my ex-husband tried to persuade me to—to have sex with another man,' she said, straightening. Then, with a complete change of expression, 'Does that feel all right?'

Demetri was stunned. But not so stunned as to allow her to turn away from him. Capturing her hand, he held onto it. To his relief, she didn't try to resist.

'Your—ex-husband?' he echoed, trying to make sense of what she'd said. 'Joanna—'

'He was gay,' she explained matter-of-factly, not looking at him. 'His parents didn't know. They would have been mortified if they had. They were fairly old, and old-fashioned. Richard was their only son, their only child. They thought he was perfect.'

Demetri's legs were splayed, and now he used his hold on her hand to tug her between them. 'Did you know?' he asked, and now she did cast another, albeit brief glance at his face.

'Not before we were married, no.'

'But—'

'I was naïve,' she said flatly. 'As I told you, I'd been brought up by an elderly aunt. Richard knew that. He used it to his own advantage.'

'Even so—'

Demetri shook his head and looked up into her troubled blue eyes. He knew he should get to his feet, but right now he was too bemused to do it. What she was saying was so incredible. *Theos*, did she expect him to believe her? Did he believe her?

'You don't believe me?'

For a moment he thought he'd spoken his thoughts out loud, but he knew as soon as he saw her doubtful features that she was merely anticipating his reaction.

'I—did not say that,' he began, but she wouldn't let him finish.

'You didn't have to,' she retorted. A bitter smile crossed her face. 'Richard's parents didn't either.'

Demetri looked down, gathering her other hand so that he held both of hers between his. 'I still do not understand,' he said softly. 'What possible satisfaction could this man get from—?'

'He wanted me to have a baby,' she answered without hesitation. 'It's ironic, really. I'd virtually resigned myself to a sterile marriage, but his parents wanted a grandchild, so...'

Demetri tilted his head to look up at her again. Was it true? Was it possible? Had he been totally wrong about her? He didn't know. What he did know was that his body was treacherously weak where she was concerned.

'And—did he succeed?' he asked, hardly wanting to hear the answer. She had said she had no children, and now he thought he could understand her reaction when he'd questioned her. But that didn't mean—

Her response was as unexpected as her revelations had been. Instead of indulging in some tedious explanation, which he might or might not have listened to, she slid her fingers between his. Then, drawing his hands aside, she stooped to brush a feather-light kiss across his startled mouth.

CHAPTER TWELVE

How Demetri prevented himself from falling back into the bath he never knew. At the touch of her lips his limbs felt boneless, and it would have been so easy to lose what little hold on reality he had. Need, hot and powerful, transmitted itself from her to him, and this time when he reached for her it was in the certain knowledge that she wouldn't push him away.

Between his legs, he'd hardened instinctively, and when her thigh brushed against the swelling in his pants he realised how totally she overwhelmed his senses—and his sanity. With his hand behind her head he crushed her mouth to his, letting her feel the hunger in his kiss. And she met his demand, her lips parting eagerly, inviting the urgent invasion of his tongue.

But Demetri wanted to feel more of her than her hands and the undoubted delight of her mouth. He wanted to feel those full rounded breasts against his chest, her nipples probing the dark hair that arrowed down to his navel. He wanted to touch her breasts, not through the fine silk, as he was doing now, but her naked breasts, warm beneath his hand. He wanted to touch her navel, too, to lick his way down her body to the soft curls he knew he'd find between her legs. *Theos*, he wanted all of her, and he was fairly sure she wanted all of him, too.

With his mouth still glued to hers, he got unsteadily to his feet, releasing her hands to cup her upper arms with fingers that were slippery with sweat. *Khristo*, no woman had ever done to him what Joanna was doing to him, and he hadn't even got her into bed yet.

But he would. He had to. And if the insistent voice of his conscience was protesting that this was his father's woman, his father's mistress, not his, he refused to listen.

Gathering her against him, he slid his fingers into the silken glory of her hair, revelling in the way it clung to his skin. Everything about her was soft and sweet and desirable, and dizziness assailed him as he edged her back into the bedroom.

It was lucky that the bed wasn't far away. He sensed the moment the back of her legs hit the side of it, and she made an unwary sound against his mouth as she lost her balance. Demetri bore her down onto the tumbled sheets, half afraid of what she might do now that his intention was clear. But to his relief she abandoned any attempt to break away from him, winding her slim arms about his neck and giving herself up to his searching caress.

Dear God. Demetri groaned, feeling the curving form beneath him. Never had a woman felt this good; never had he been so desperate to make love. The cord of the negligee had loosened in her fall, and now all that was between his hand and the sensuous touch of her skin was the virtually transparent fabric of her nightgown. He wanted to tear it from her, to expose the enchanting length of her to his hungry gaze. But, remembering what she had said earlier, he controlled his wilder impulses. There was no hurry, he told himself unsteadily. They had the rest of the night.

Although he was half afraid that in freeing her mouth he might give her the chance to change her mind, the simple need for oxygen had him releasing her lips to bury his face in the scented hollow of her throat. His heart was hammering like a mad thing in his chest and he gulped air into his starved lungs.

But Joanna had her own agenda, he discovered. Her fingers curled into the hair at his nape, pressing his face against her, inciting a need in his lower limbs that was almost impossible to control. One slim leg curved across his thigh and a seductively bare sole inched beneath the cuff of his pants and caressed his ankle.

Demetri's blood pounded through his veins. He wanted out of his clothes, and fast. With unsteady fingers he tore at the buckle of his belt, struggling with the button on his pants that arrantly refused to come loose. Then slim fingers brushed his hands aside, and seconds later he felt the relief of his zip sliding virtually unassisted over his pulsing erection.

He half hoped she would go on and finish the job, but she didn't. With a breathless little gasp she pulled her hand away, and he was obliged to jerk the trousers over his hips and kick them off. His tee shirt followed them, and this time her reaction was much more positive. Almost tentatively, it seemed, her fingers probed the fine growth of hair that covered his chest, her nails finding his nipples before she rolled them beneath her palms.

Demetri couldn't wait much longer. Unable to stop himself, he found the hem of her nightgown and drew it up to her waist. Long legs, a deliciously flat abdomen, the hollow of her navel: he saw all this in a moment. But his eyes moved swiftly to the cluster of pale curls between her legs, and, as if aware of where his attention was focussed, she shifted almost nervously beneath his gaze.

'Theos, is' oreos!' God, you're beautiful! His throat constricted with unaccustomed emotion. 'Ah, Joanna, do you have any idea how much I want you?'

Her lips parted. 'Do you?' she asked, her voice barely more than a whisper. 'Do you really want me? Or—or—?'

'Or nothing,' he said hoarsely, peeling her nightgown over her head as he spoke. His eyes darkened at the sight of her breasts, full and swollen and as rosily perfect as he had anticipated. With a shuddering sigh he bent to take one tight nipple into his mouth. He wet it with his tongue, his teeth digging ever so gently into the soft skin that surrounded it. Then, speaking against her flesh, 'How could you doubt it?'

'You—you could have any woman you wanted,' she protested, her nails digging into his shoulders, and he gave a shuddering sigh.

'I do not want any other woman,' he told her unevenly, and knew amazingly that it was true. 'I just want you.'

'But—'

There was only one way to silence her and he used it. Even as his hand slid down over the quivering swell of her belly to find the moist core of her womanhood his lips closed over hers again, his tongue plunging possessively into her mouth.

She opened to him with delicious eagerness, capturing his tongue between her teeth as she opened her legs to admit his probing fingers.

She was ready for him. Her essence wet his fingers, rose in sensual waves of heat and urgency to his nose. And she was tight; so tight that it would be incredibly easy to delude himself that no other man had ever possessed her. She bucked a little as he caressed her, increasing the notion that no man had done this before.

He stifled a moan of impatience, realising he was in danger of losing what little control he had. Her fingers were on his back, exploring his backbone. Then sliding beneath the waistband of his shorts, finding the cleft between his buttocks with mind-shuddering intimacy.

She had no idea how close he was to making a complete fool of himself, he thought dazedly. But she must have. She was no teenager, indulging in her first experiment with sex. She was a mature woman, adult and experienced. She must know exactly what her teasing hands were doing to him.

'My God, Joanna,' he said hoarsely, feeling his shorts snag on his erection. Cool air was a relief against his hot flesh, and somehow he got the shorts down his legs so he could kick them off. He heard her breath catch in her throat when she saw him, and once again he had that feeling of unreality. But she was all woman. She was warm and sexy, and so responsive that she blew his mind.

Taking one of her hands, he deliberately brought it to him. Balancing his control on a knife-edge, he encouraged her fingers to close around him, and gave a groan of protest when she did as he asked.

'What is it? Did I do something wrong?' she murmured anxiously, drawing her hand away again, and he uttered a strangled gasp.

'No,' he assured her huskily. 'You did everything right. It's—oh, *Theos*. I want to love you, Joanna. Let me really love you. Let me show you how incredible you are.'

She rose up then, to cover his lips with hers, and this time it was her tongue that surged into his mouth. Her kiss drove all thoughts of anything—or anybody—else out of his head. Her breasts were crushed against his chest; her stomach was close against his abdomen. Her spread legs, with knees drawn up, made it easy for him to move between her thighs.

He ached with the needs she had aroused in him. Looking down, seeing himself poised at the moist opening to her body, he didn't know how he stopped himself from simply plunging into her enticing heat. He wanted to. God, how he wanted to. Even the knowledge that he had come unprepared for such intimacy was no real deterrent. But something, some inner instinct, perhaps, urged him to take his time.

He'd have liked to explain it as a belated sense of honour that had given him pause. But that wasn't true. He was too obsessed with her, with his own passion for her, to entertain any serious doubts about what he was doing now. He wanted her. He was going to have her. But perhaps it would be good to prolong the expectation.

Good—but hardly sensible. Just the touch of her warmth, of her woman's body, had him trembling like a schoolboy. Senses were heightened, needs refined. This was going to be a life-altering experience. He didn't know how he knew that, but he did.

She was tight, so tight, he thought again. That was his final thought as he eased closer. Making love to her was going to be like making love to a virgin, and he hadn't known many of those in his career.

Her muscles closed about him, gripped him, driving him almost to a climax with their rippling strength. She was amazing, he thought, in his last coherent moment before his control snapped. Having her once was never going to be enough...

*   *   *

Joanna tensed. She couldn't help herself. So far, Demetri's hands and lips and tongue had done a wonderful job of convincing her that she could do this, but suddenly she wasn't so sure. She wasn't what he expected, and although she'd persuaded herself that he need never know how inexperienced she was, that proposition no longer sounded so feasible.

Doubts flooded her mind: doubts about Demetri's real intentions, doubts about what she was doing. Even now she could hardly conceive of how she'd got herself into this situation, and the hot blood swept into her throat at the realisation of how wantonly she had behaved.

Was behaving, she amended unsteadily, trying to draw her legs together and finding the way blocked by hard, muscular thighs. Oh, God, he was really going to do it. He was going to have sex with her. Already she could feel the blunt heat of him nudging the sensitive place between her legs. And while the intelligent part of her brain was telling her that she couldn't go through with this, another part, a reckless emotional entity, was urging her to give in to the needs that even sanity couldn't deny.

She was shaking. More from anticipation than fear, she acknowledged weakly. But that didn't make it right. Yet she couldn't deny that she had started this. It was she who had kissed Demetri; she who had allowed him to push her down onto the bed and make a mockery of the frigidity she had always wrapped around her like a shield.

What was different about Demetri? Why, when she'd seen him standing beside her bed, hadn't she done what any sensible woman would have done and called for help? He'd had his back to her, after all, and just because *she'd* known instantly who it was, no one else would have doubted her panic at finding a dark-clad intruder in her room.

But she hadn't done that. In fact she'd been almost apologetic when he'd asked her where she'd been. Nor had she explained why she had been in Constantine's room. She had no doubt Demetri thought she'd come straight from his father's bed, but of course she hadn't. She'd been in her own bed when she'd felt the need to check on Constantine, and she'd been returning from that unnecessary expedition when she'd found Demetri in circumstances which could only be described as suspicious.

Yet she'd accepted his explanation that he'd wanted to finish the conversation they'd been having when Athenee had interrupted them. A thin explanation at best, she conceded now, when they'd both known that talking was not what

Demetri had had in mind. Then or now, she appended silently, her head swimming with so many wild emotions she could hardly think.

So what was different about Demetri? she asked herself again, trying to hold on to her own identity. Why, when Demetri kissed her, when he caressed her, when he crushed her beneath his heavy muscular body, didn't she remember how it had been with Richard? Why didn't she freeze up, as she had with every other man since her ex-husband had made such a travesty of her life?

She didn't know the answer. She only knew that Demetri aroused her in ways she'd never been aroused before. He made her feel like a woman, a real woman. A desirable woman, moreover. Without even being aware of it he had given her back her self-respect. And although she suspected she wouldn't feel half so positive in the morning, right now she didn't have the will—or the strength—to resist him.

However, that still didn't solve the problem of what she ought to do *now*. Though when Demetri sucked in his breath and dipped his head to lave her nipples with his tongue she found she was too bemused to care.

'You are—*apithanos*! Incredible,' he told her thickly, and all thought of trying to explain herself disappeared.

'Am I?' she heard herself say breathily, and instead of drawing away, telling him that he'd made a mistake about her, she arched up to meet him.

And knew at once that it was too late. The thick shaft which she had glimpsed earlier—and which had caused her no small measure of apprehension—was already pushing past the tight muscles that guarded her womb.

Heat, hot and hard and throbbing with life, was invading her lower body. It wasn't painful, but it was unfamiliar, and she knew a moment's consternation that she wouldn't be able to go on. Richard had not been particularly well-endowed, whereas Demetri was—was—

The pain that tore through her at that moment drove any thought of her ex-husband out of her head. Sharp and unexpected, it stifled the breath in her throat and brought hot tears to her eyes. She couldn't prevent the cry that broke from her lips at that moment, and if he had had any doubts before, Demetri was instantly aware of what he had done.

His eyes, suddenly burning into hers, were dark with confusion. And although it was much too late for him to do anything about it, it was obvious he was as shocked as she was. She felt his erection partially subside, and he shook his head as if to clear it. Then he stared at her as if he'd never seen her before.

'*Theos,*' he said in a shaken voice, his hands coming to cup her face. '*Mou lete*—that is, why did you not tell me?'

Joanna was flushed, as much from humiliation as anything else. But inside she felt cold. This was not how it was supposed to turn out. What price now her foolish hopes of hiding her ignorance from him?

'W-would you have believed me?' she asked at last, and Demetri acknowledged the guarded accusation with a rueful nod of his head.

'*Ala*—but you were married!' he exclaimed blankly, and she sighed.

'I told you about that.'

'Obviously not enough,' he said wryly, looking down to where their bodies were still joined. He uttered an oath. '*Signomi*. I am sorry. I should never have done this.'

Joanna's eyes darted to his then, the realisation that this might be her only chance to at least pretend she was like any other woman making her reckless. 'Do you regret coming here?' she breathed, sliding her hands up his chest. Once more she felt him stir inside her. 'You said you wanted me.'

'I did not know,' he said hoarsely, grasping her hands in his to prevent their caressing touch. 'Joanna, you must understand that— Ah, *Khristo*—my father!' He shook his head dazedly. 'I do not understand.'

'Do you have to?' she protested, managing to reach his flat stomach with her fingertips. She gazed up at him. 'Not now, please!' Her tongue appeared in innocent provocation. 'Demetri: make love to me.'

'*Mou Theos*, Joanna…'

The muscles in his wrists tensed as he endeavoured to restrain her. But he didn't try very hard, and it was comparatively easy for her to break free and link her hands about his neck.

Her fingers tangled in the moist hair at his nape, and she exulted in the knowledge that she had done this to him. 'Kiss me,' she said, discovering a confidence in herself she'd never known before. She reached up to him, finding his breathless mouth with hers, and with another muffled oath he cradled her face between his palms and returned the kiss.

The magic had returned. A thrill of excitement swept over her trembling limbs, sending the blood pounding through her veins. She was no longer afraid of what was to happen. She welcomed it as she welcomed the undoubted strength of his passion. Emotions, wild and turbulent, had taken over, and she was all softness, all eagerness, all woman in his arms.

Demetri couldn't resist her. Joanna seemed to know instinctively how to please him. Her teeth dug into his shoulder, drawing a groan of pleasurable protest from him, and then her hands curved over his tight buttocks, bringing him even more fully between her thighs.

The only protest she made was when she thought he was going to draw away from her. But he came into her again, more powerfully than before, and where earlier there had been a nervous frisson of feeling, now she felt a stirring need that was tantalisingly different.

The muscles that gripped him tightened almost automatically, and Demetri slid his hands beneath her to lift her to his thrusting shaft. He said something she didn't understand, some unsteady words in his own language whose meaning was perfectly clear nevertheless, and then added huskily, 'You have no idea how much I have wanted this— wanted you. Dear heaven, you have driven me— crazy!'

She wanted to say, Me, too, but she couldn't. A rising crescendo of need seemed to be building inside her, and only incoherent sounds of both pleasure and protest were issuing from her lips.

She wanted to say that it couldn't go on, that *she* couldn't stand it, but apparently she could. Demetri's increasingly urgent body was plunging wildly into hers, and, looking up into his driven, sweating face, she saw a need to match her own.

His eyes were wide, impassioned, and her hands sought the damp skin of his shoulders in a desperate need to anchor herself. She had the feeling she was losing herself, losing her sanity, gradually being absorbed into the being that was him.

Her climax came suddenly. It was as if she had been striving for something that was always out of reach and abruptly found it within her grasp. Shuddering ripples of pleasure swept over her quivering body, and for a few incredible moments she was totally blown away. It was like nothing she had ever felt before, nothing she could ever have imagined, and it took an effort to focus her eyes again and look at Demetri.

He, too, was caught up in the moment. Even as she watched he thrust violently against her, and she felt the flooding warmth of what could only be his seed inside her. *His seed!* Dear heaven, she wasn't on the pill. She could get pregnant. Imagine how he would feel if she found she was carrying his child.

But she had no time to consider those implications. Even as Demetri collapsed upon her, even as he gave himself up to the luxury of pillowing his head in the dusky hollow between her breasts, they both heard the sound of a man's voice from the sitting room next door.

'*Kiria!* Kiria Manning!' called Philip's anxious tones, and Joanna stiffened. 'Kirie Constantine calls for you, *kiria*. I am afraid he is not well.'

CHAPTER THIRTEEN

DEMETRI stood beside his father's bed, watching the old man sleep. The private hospital on the outskirts of Athens was not where he wished his father to be. Not where *he* wished to be, if it came to that. But so long as Constantine's health was a cause for concern it was the only place he could be.

And his father was much better. Despite the tubes and wires to which he was still attached, the doctors had assured him that the old man's condition was stable. As stable as it could be, bearing in mind that his father was dying from terminal cancer.

Demetri's stomach hollowed. He knew now that the operation his father had had performed in the London hospital had not been the success he'd told his family it was. Indeed, Constantine had only had the operation in London because he'd been warned by his doctors in Athens that it was already too late for invasive surgery. The stomach cancer had spread to his other organs. Only in a foreign hospital could he hope to keep his condition from his children. And he'd wanted to do that because of Alex. Because he'd had no intention of being the spectre at his youngest daughter's wedding feast.

Demetri expelled a weary breath. He'd believed him, he thought incredulously. When he'd visited him in London his father had always been unfailingly upbeat about his treatment. Even the doctor in charge of his case had apparently been warned not to relay any unpleasant details to the family until after Alex's wedding. As far as they'd been concerned, the treatment he'd received had been successful. After the usual period of convalescence Constantine would be cured.

Demetri's jaw compressed. He realised now why his father had brought Joanna with him when he'd returned to the island. He'd guessed that, without her distracting presence, his children might have been more inclined to question his recovery. It was only because he'd behaved like a besotted old man that they'd overlooked the inconsistencies of his condition. The fact that he'd apparently felt well enough to entertain a much younger woman had blinded them to the truth. They'd believed what he'd wanted them to believe, Demetri conceded heavily. They'd been totally deceived, and that had been Constantine's intention all along.

But Demetri knew the truth now. Shaking his head, he moved to the windows that looked out onto the formal gardens that surrounded the hospital. Beyond manicured lawns, the blue-grey waters of the Aegean surged constantly. It had been raining earlier in the day, and the sea below the cliffs upon which the hospital was situated was still shrouded in mist. Somewhere out there was Theapolis, Demetri mused grimly. How long was it going to be before his father could return to the island? Before *he* could do the same? How long before they could both go home?

His fists clenched at his sides. He needed to go home, he thought impatiently. However painful it was going to be, he needed to talk to Joanna again. Whatever else, he needed to see her. God alone knew, he owed her that much.

It had been three long days and three even longer nights since he and his father had flown from Agios Antonis to Athens. Daniil Tsikas had accompanied them. The island doctor, whom Demetri had summoned as soon as he'd seen his father and realised the old man was having difficulty in breathing, had lost no time in contacting the hospital in Athens and arranging for his patient's emergency admission.

Constantine had been conscious when the arrangements were being made and he'd expressed his objections. He'd insisted he only needed his medication, but Demetri hadn't listened to him. He'd needed a professional opinion, a specialist's opinion, and when he'd learned how ill his father really was he'd realised why the old man had tried to stop him.

Stubborn old fool, Demetri thought now, fighting the unwelcome prick of tears behind his eyes. Dammit, he could have told him; he *should* have told him. He was his father's only son; his heir. He had the right to know what was going on.

Joanna had known. His mouth tightened as he accepted the fact that Joanna had known all along. She had been in his father's confidence. He couldn't have done it without her. And that was something Demetri was finding incredibly hard to swallow.

Yet how could he blame her for something that had been his father's decision? It wasn't her fault that Constantine had chosen to pretend he'd recovered. The fact that she'd gone along with it was surely incidental. But what had she got out of it? What did she expect to get out of it? She hadn't even shared his father's bed.

Thank God!

His hands clenched into fists at his sides. He wondered what she was thinking now. Would she be pleased to see him again? He thrust his fists into the pockets of his leather jacket. Somehow he doubted it. He couldn't help remembering the expression on her face when she'd heard his father's old manservant calling to her from the sitting room of her apartments. There'd been regret there, and remorse. And a certain bitterness. Whatever she'd been thinking, she hadn't said a word. She'd simply fought her way free of him, snatched up her robe and pulled it on before leaving the room.

Of course since then he'd had time to consider the reasons for her behaviour. It was possible that she'd wanted to save him any embarrassment. It was true that by leaving the bedroom she'd prevented Philip from seeing him. It had been a simple matter for him to throw on his clothes and follow her. Philip had accepted his appearance in his father's bedroom without any suspicion. But then, they'd all been too concerned about Constantine's condition to care about anything else.

It wasn't until much later that Demetri had had the chance to wonder what would have happened if Philip hadn't interrupted them. The whole experience had been eclipsed by what had come after, and although there'd been times when he'd told himself it was all for the best, that what had happened had been the result of over-stimulated emotions and too much champagne, it didn't always work.

They hadn't had too much champagne that day at the temple, and he couldn't deny that he'd wanted her then, too. Indeed, if he was honest, he would have to admit that he'd wanted her ever since she'd first challenged him with those incredibly sexy eyes. Seeing her with his father, believing they were lovers, had torn him to pieces. So much so that he'd been prepared to betray the old man if he could have her himself.

Which was something he couldn't forgive.

Couldn't forgive himself, anyway, he amended. Joanna had done nothing wrong. Not really. Apart from exposing the charade of her supposed affair with his father, she'd committed no crime. Whereas he...

He turned back to the bed and gazed at Constantine's drawn face with a terrible feeling of remorse in his soul. What kind of a son was he to do such a thing? How could he live with himself, knowing that if Joanna *had* been his father's mistress he'd have broken the old man's heart.

So why did he want to see Joanna again? What did he think could be achieved by talking to her? No doubt she despised him, too. That would explain her reaction when Philip had come crying for her help.

She'd phoned every day since Constantine had been admitted to the hospital. Demetri hadn't spoken to her, but the nurses, who were all thrilled to have such an important patient in the hospital, were always eager to convey every concerned enquiry to either himself or Olivia.

His sister was here, of course. Olivia had arrived the morning after their father's emergency admission, chiding Demetri for not waking her and telling her that the old man had been taken ill in the night. She'd berated Joanna, too, for being the undoubted cause of their father's relapse. Even hearing the facts of Constantine's condition from the consultant oncologist hadn't altered her opinion that the demands Joanna had made must have precipitated his collapse. And Demetri hadn't been able to contradict her without involving himself.

He couldn't do that. Not without betraying his father again. So long as the old man wanted them to believe that Joanna really was his mistress he couldn't do anything to refute his claim. Okay, maybe he had his own reasons for not wanting to admit what a bastard he really was, but that was only a temporary reprieve. Sooner or later he was going to have to confess his sins to the family.

Yet why? he asked himself bitterly. What would his confession achieve? Olivia would despise him and even Alex would find it hard to forgive him. It wasn't as if Joanna was going to feel any pride in him baring his soul. The fact that she'd made no attempt to come to the hospital proved that she had no desire to see him again.

His father stirred, and, leaving the window, Demetri approached the bed. The old man looked so frail, he thought uneasily. Makarios, the consultant in charge of his father's case, had admitted that he couldn't give them any guarantees of how much longer he might have. Constantine was already living on borrowed time.

'Demetri?'

His voice was frail, too, and Demetri had to stifle the oath of frustration that sprang to his lips. If only money could buy his father a little more time, he thought despairingly. He'd gladly sacrifice the whole Kastro fortune in his cause.

'I am here, Papa,' he said now, moving closer. 'How are you feeling?'

'Much better,' said Constantine firmly, even though his son knew that couldn't possibly be true. 'Is Joanna outside?'

It wasn't the first time his father had asked for Joanna, but so far Olivia had been able to put him off with excuses as to why she wasn't there. His sister absolutely refused to allow Joanna to be treated as part of the family, and Demetri was now obliged to continue the deception.

'I am sure she would like to be,' he said, knowing as he spoke that his father would put his own interpretation on her absence. 'The weather has been bad since you left the island. Roussos has not been willing to take the helicopter up in such conditions.'

'In other words, you have not permitted her to come,' declared Constantine wearily, and Demetri thought it was par for the course that he should be the one to take the blame. His father hadn't accused Olivia. Only him.

'That is not true,' he insisted. Then, defensively, 'There are other methods of transportation. Ferries, for example.'

He was tempted to go on and say that if she'd really wanted to come she'd have made her own way to Athens, but that would have been too cruel. But it was true, he reflected broodingly. Joanna didn't know that Olivia had taken up guard outside their father's room.

Constantine was not to be put off, however. 'Do not pretend that you would welcome her here,' he exclaimed, and Demetri was alarmed to see the sudden hectic colour that filled the old man's cheeks. 'Nurse Delos tells me she has phoned many times. Is it so hard for you to understand that I want to see her?'

'No.' Demetri conceded the point, aware that his own pulse-rate had quickened at the thought of seeing her again. But his feelings were not important. 'I will see what I can do.'

'Good. Good.' To his relief his father seemed satisfied with his reply. He licked his dry lips. 'I need a drink.'

Demetri stepped forward and lifted a glass from the bedside cabinet, inserting the straw it held into his father's mouth. The old man sucked and a little of the liquid disappeared. 'Thank you.'

Demetri returned the glass to the cabinet and forced a smile. 'I will leave you to rest,' he said, realising that even this brief conversation had tired him. 'I will come back later.'

'I suppose you think I should have told you that I am dying.'

Constantine's words startled him, and Demetri, who had started for the door, turned back. 'Papa—'

'Do not deny it, Demetri.' His father's chest rose and fell with the force of his agitation. 'But do not blame Joanna because I did not.'

Demetri shook his head. This was the first occasion that Constantine had mentioned his illness and he didn't know how to answer him. Until now his father had been too ill to indulge in any serious discussion of his condition, and he didn't want to say anything to upset him.

'I do not blame her,' he replied at last, coming back to the bed. 'I—accept that you had your reasons for doing what you did.'

Constantine's parched lips twitched. 'You are very understanding. That is not like you, Demetri. Do not let this momentary relapse fool you. I will be up and about again before very long and you may wish you had been more honest with me.'

Demetri gave a small smile. 'I think you should rest, Papa.'

'And I will.' Constantine groped towards him and nodded in satisfaction when his son put his hand into his. 'When you assure me that you will make your peace with Joanna.'

'Make my peace with—'

Demetri was confused, but his father wasn't finished. 'You know what I am talking about, *mi yos*. I saw the way you looked at her the night I was taken ill. You thought I would not notice—' Demetri stiffened '—but I could see that you disliked her being there, disliked the role that she was playing. Do you resent her, Demetri? If so, that is a pity, because I had hoped that you two would become friends.'

Friends! Demetri felt a constriction in his chest. If only that were true.

'Papa—' he began, but once again his father forestalled him.

'She has not had an easy life, Demetri,' he said, closing his eyes as if the effort of talking exhausted him. 'Her husband—ex-husband—was totally unsuitable. I cannot go into personal details except to say that he made her very unhappy.'

Demetri inclined his head. 'I understand.'

'I doubt you do.' Constantine held up a trembling hand. 'He hurt and humiliated her, Demetri. He took away every shred of self-respect she had. When I first got to know her she was shy and uncommunicative. She had lost all confidence in herself as an attractive woman.' He paused and opened his eyes again. 'I like to think I changed all that. Slowly, but surely, she opened up to me. We became friends, and when I was first advised of the terminality of my illness it was she I could talk to, she who offered the comfort I could not ask of my own family.'

Demetri sighed. 'Papa—'

'No. Hear me out, Demetri. She is not what you think.' He expelled a weary breath. 'She is a decent woman, Demetri. And I care about her.'

He looked at his son with heavy-lidded eyes. 'Do you understand? I care about her.'

Demetri was very still. 'Why are you telling me this, Papa?' Dear God, was the old man saying he wanted to marry her?

'Because I love her, Demetri,' Constantine replied. 'Because she is dear to me. Because when I am dead I want you to promise me that you will see that she never wants for anything again.'

'No! No, I will not allow it!'

Olivia faced her brother in the ante-room that adjoined their father's suite, her face flushed with anger. Demetri thought it was just as well that all the rooms in the hospital were soundproofed. He could be fairly certain that Constantine wouldn't hear what was going on.

Nevertheless, her obstinacy infuriated him. 'Keep your voice down,' he snapped. 'Do you want everybody to hear that we are already quarrelling over his wishes? It is our father's desire that Joanna should be brought to the hospital. That is all there is to it.'

Olivia snorted. 'His desire, yes. We know all about our father's desires, do we not?'

'Olivia—'

'No, do not attempt to justify this, Demetri.' She wrapped her arms about her waist and stared at him with bitter eyes. 'Why did you not tell him she has gone back to England? Why did you let him think that she is waiting at the villa, anticipating the day when he will return to Theapolis?'

Demetri schooled his features before replying. 'Just because you do not like her—'

Olivia caught her breath. 'Are you saying that you do?'

Off-guard, Demetri was more outspoken than he should have been. 'She is not as bad as you think,' he said sharply. 'At least she cares about the old man.'

'I do not believe this.' Olivia's eyes narrowed. 'She has bewitched you as well as Papa.' She shook her head. 'I warned you what she was like, but you wouldn't listen.'

'You are imagining things,' retorted Demetri, hoping against hope that it was true. 'All I am saying is that you should give her the benefit of the doubt, Olivia. Or do you think our father is such a poor judge of character?'

Olivia wasn't having that. 'I do not think a man in his condition is capable of making rational judgements,' she declared. 'I always wondered why she had taken up with him. Well, now I know. She knew he was ill. She knew exactly how long she would have to play her part.'

'*Siopi!*' Be quiet! Demetri had had quite enough of her vitriolic comments. 'It was not like that. Joanna has known our father for a number of years. Long before—long before he discovered he had a tumour.'

'You believe that?'

'It is the truth.'

'Because she told you so?'

'No, because he did,' Demetri replied heavily. 'Now, if you will excuse me, I am going to ring the villa and arrange for Joanna's transportation to Athens.'

Olivia took a resentful breath. And then she said carelessly, 'She is not there.'

Time seemed to stand still for a moment, and Demetri had to force himself to say, 'What do you mean? She is not there?'

'What is there about that sentence you do not understand?' Olivia enquired coldly. 'Read my lips, Demetri. Joanna is not at the villa. She has gone back to London.'

Demetri mentally shook himself. Joanna had gone back to London? He couldn't believe it. 'When? When did she leave?'

Olivia shrugged. 'Three days ago.'

Demetri blinked. 'But she has phoned every day.'

'I imagine the telecommunications system in England is just as efficient as ours,' said Olivia dismissively, and he felt a violent urge to shake her, too.

Stepping close to her, he said malevolently, 'Am I to understand that you are responsible for her departure?'

For the first time, Olivia looked a little uneasy. 'So—so what if I am?' she asked defensively. 'It is surely what you would have done if you had not been here with our father.'

Demetri scowled. 'If you think that, Olivia, why are you looking so uncertain now?' He was amazed at how furious he felt that she should have done this. 'You—' He heard a faint tremor in his voice and determinedly suppressed it. 'You—had no right!'

'I had every right,' retorted Olivia indignantly. 'You know she was to blame for Papa's relapse. If she hadn't been making—unreasonable demands on his strength, he would not have been so weak when—'

'She was not his mistress!' snarled Demetri, stung into the involuntary admission, and Olivia's hands dropped to her sides.

'Not his mistress?' she echoed faintly. Then, more certainly, 'How do you know?'

How did he know?

Demetri returned her gaze with a flat stare. 'I just do,' he said at last, not prepared to lie even to save himself.

Olivia's lips parted. 'Papa told you?' she prompted.

'No.' Demetri spoke dispassionately. 'Papa did not tell me.'

'You do not mean to say that you believe her lies?' his sister cried scornfully. 'Demetri—'

'Joanna did not lie. Nor did she have to tell me anything,' he grated, through his teeth. 'Do I need to draw a picture?'

Olivia clapped her hands to her cheeks. 'You— you— Oh, I do not believe this.' She took a step back from him, her eyes wide with dismay. 'You—you had sex with her?' She seemed to take his silence as an answer. 'Then surely that only proves the kind of woman she is.'

'She was a virgin, Olivia,' Demetri told her harshly. 'Yes, a virgin.' This as Olivia tried to speak. 'So when you next feel the need to vilify Joanna, I think you should beware of what you say.'

CHAPTER FOURTEEN

THE light was flashing on the answering machine when Joanna got home from work. Her heart skipped a nervous beat. She'd left her number with the hospital in Athens, asking them to let her know if there was any change in Constantine's condition. The few friends she had usually called in the evenings, so who else could it be?

She hurried across the small living room of the apartment and pressed the 'play' button. Then she waited, praying that it wasn't bad news. She didn't think she could take any more bad news right now.

It wasn't the hospital. The voice issuing from the recorder was far too familiar, and she missed the start of the message as she groped for the arm of the nearest chair and sank down onto it. Her legs were shaking as she wondered with a feeling of dismay if Constantine had died. It was the only reason she could think of why Demetri might be phoning her.

'—sister told me how it was,' he was saying, his voice clipped but not unfriendly. 'No matter. My father is asking for you. We would all be very grateful if you could arrange to return to Greece immediately.'

The message cut off and Joanna sat staring at the light that was still flashing for several seconds before switching it off. Then, panicking because she hadn't heard the entire message, she pressed the wrong button and had to sit through half a dozen old messages before hearing Demetri's voice again.

She hadn't missed much. Just, 'Joanna,' and, 'I'm sorry you felt you had to return to England.' She'd tuned in at the point when he'd been saying that his sister had told him how it was, and Joanna pulled a wry face. Knowing Olivia as she did, she doubted she'd been completely honest about their encounter. The Greek girl had been very unpleasant, accusing Joanna of endangering her father's life and ordering her to leave the villa.

Nevertheless, the import of Demetri's message was clear. Constantine wanted to see her and, willing or not, Olivia was being forced to eat her words.

Joanna drew a trembling breath. It wasn't Olivia's reaction that troubled her. If even the sound of his voice could make her legs weak, how on earth was she going to meet Demetri again and behave as if nothing had changed? Because of course it had. For her, at least. Nothing in her life was ever going to be the same again.

In fact, that was why she hadn't taken a stand against Olivia. Spiro, who had been given the task of seeing Joanna off the island, had urged her to wait until Demetri got back. He'd insisted that he was in touch with Demetri every day and that his employer wouldn't be pleased if she returned to London.

But Joanna had insisted on leaving. A small private plane had flown her to Athens, and she'd boarded the London flight there. In a matter of hours after Constantine's collapse she'd been back in her own apartment. If it hadn't been for the rack of totally unsuitable clothes hanging in her wardrobe she might have been able to convince herself that it had all been a bad dream.

Right.

She pulled a wry face. The chance of her being able to put what had happened out of her mind wasn't even an option. The memories were far too real, far too acute. She was never going to be able to forget what had happened. She wasn't sure she even wanted to.

Which was crazy, she knew. Oh, Demetri might have felt some remorse at having misjudged her so completely, but she wasn't fool enough to think that that passionate interlude in her bedroom had meant anything to him. He'd wanted her. He'd told her that. But wanting didn't equal loving, and nothing that had happened between them was going to make the slightest difference to the plans he had for his future. Even Constantine had made it perfectly clear that he expected his son to marry a woman of his own nationality.

Marry!

Joanna caught her breath. Now where had that come from? She must be going senile if she was associating a sexual affair with marriage. As far as she knew Demetri was in no hurry to marry anyone, but when he did decide to make that kind of commitment he would make sure the woman he chose was completely without a flaw. Certainly not someone who had already been dismissed as his father's mistress.

She sighed, not at all sure what she was going to do. She wanted to see Constantine again; of course she did. She would do anything for the man who had been like a father to her; who had been there for her when she'd needed him; who had helped her to get her divorce from Richard. Without him she might still have been married to that creep; might still have been finding excuses why she shouldn't tell his parents what he was really like.

Her association with Constantine had had such an unlikely beginning, she reflected now. When her boss, Martin Scott, had asked her to deliver a Fabergé snuffbox to one of their most important clients at the Grosvenor Park Hotel, she'd had no idea that she and Constantine would become such friends. But the Greek tycoon had taken an immediate liking to the shy English girl, and although it had taken many months and many more deliveries to his hotel for them to get to know one another, they had gradually become close.

Maybe Constantine had guessed how unhappy she was, Joanna mused, walking into the neat kitchen that adjoined the living space. Or maybe she had just needed someone to talk to, someone who could give her an objective opinion of what had been going on.

In any event, it was to Constantine she had confessed the travesty of her marriage, Constantine who had offered the advice that she should cut her losses and start again.

But that had been easier said than done. Richard had been a master manipulator, and for a long time he had controlled her with threats of what he would do if she left him.

He must have really believed she would never leave him, she thought, carrying the kettle to the sink and filling it from the tap. He must have convinced himself that she was too submissive, too scared to break out on her own. She doubted he would otherwise have dared to bring a string of strange men to their apartment, leaving her alone with them, hoping that she would find one of them attractive enough to go to bed with...

Joanna shivered. Richard had been wrong. With Constantine's support she had gone to see a solicitor and in a short space of time she had moved out of the apartment. Through all the murky days that had followed he had been there for her; the days when Richard's parents had accused her of ruining their son's life. And when she'd finally got her divorce it had been Constantine who had warned Richard not to try and see her again, Constantine who had shared her feelings of sadness and relief that it was over.

Now she looked about her a little uncertainly. Going out to Greece again would mean that she would have to behave as if nothing had happened between her and Demetri, and that wouldn't be easy. No matter how often she'd told herself that she should put it all down to experience, she wasn't that kind of woman. She could never have gone to bed with Demetri without having feelings for him. Feelings she'd fought, goodness knew, but which had only become stronger since her return.

She stood staring out of the window at the darkening street below as the kettle boiled. A row of pots stood on the windowsill, the flowering plants they contained giving a warmth and personality to the small room. Copper pans, hanging above a centre island, were reflected in the tiled walls, but Joanna was in no mood to appreciate the home she'd made for herself at the moment.

What should she do? It was possible that Constantine was worse and that that was why they'd been forced to send for her. She'd phoned the hospital in Athens that morning and been told he'd had a comfortable night, but how reliable was that? She wasn't a member of his family. Any private information would be reserved for the Kastros. They could tell her anything and she'd be none the wiser.

The kettle boiled and she made herself a pot of tea. She had planned on sending out for pizza later, if she was hungry, but now the idea of food choked her. What was she going to do?

Less than forty-eight hours later, Joanna was getting out of a taxi at the imposing entrance to the Oceanis Hospital just a short distance from Athens.

She'd taken that morning's flight from London and checked into a small hotel not far from the

Plaka before ordering a taxi to bring her here. She'd wanted to have her own base, somewhere she could escape to if things proved too difficult for her. She didn't want to be dependent on the Kastros for anything.

She hadn't tried to get in touch with Demetri. She'd had enough to do, she excused herself. It hadn't been easy getting leave of absence from her job. She'd just returned from a fortnight's holiday, after all. Then there'd been her apartment to see to. She'd had to arrange for an elderly neighbour to water the plants and take in any mail. Besides, she'd decided that as it was Constantine who had sent for her it was he, and only he, she owed any explanations to. Not that she intended to tell him anything that would upset him. He'd never hear the real reason why she'd returned to England. She was certain of that.

Automatic glass doors gave access to a marble and glass entrance hall, and Joanna approached the reception desk with some trepidation. What if Demetri wasn't here to vouch for her? she worried belatedly. She was loath to involve him, but if they refused to let her see his father she'd have to. She didn't consider Olivia. If she had her way, Joanna guessed she would be on the next plane home.

To her relief, the receptionist spoke English.

'Mrs Manning?' she queried, consulting a ledger lying on the desk in front of her. 'And you are a friend of Mr Kastro's, *ne*?'

'*Ne*—I mean, yes.' Joanna felt awkward. 'I think you'll find he's been asking to see me.'

'*Psemata!*' Joanna didn't have to understand the language to see that this glamorous young woman's raised brows and the pencil tapping thoughtfully against immaculate white teeth indicated some doubt with that assertion. 'I regret only family members are permitted to visit Mr Kastro, Mrs Manning.'

'Nevertheless—'

'I am sorry.' The woman seemed genuinely regretful now, but Joanna guessed she'd been tutored in polite refusals. If Constantine was a patient here, it followed that this was no ordinary hospital. Its staff must be used to dealing with unwelcome visitors. The media, for example. 'I cannot help you, Mrs Manning.'

Joanna heaved a breath. 'Mr Demetrios Kastro, then,' she said quickly, before she could regret the words. 'Perhaps you could tell him I'm here.'

The receptionist regarded her a little impatiently now. 'Mrs Manning—'

'You don't understand.' Joanna was getting frantic. 'I really am a friend of Mr Constantine Kastro. Ask—ask any of his family.'

The sudden presence of a man at her elbow startled her. For a moment she thought Demetri had heard she was here and had come to her rescue, but the man standing beside her was a stranger to her. He was also wearing a uniform that Joanna recognised as matching that worn by the receptionist, but the bulge beneath the left side of his jacket was definitely different. And scary.

'*Apo etho ineh, kiria,*' he said, gesturing towards the glass doors, and Joanna realised he was asking her to leave.

'You don't understand—' she began again, but it was too late. The man had placed his hand beneath her elbow and was gently but firmly drawing her away from the desk.

She was going to have to leave, she thought unhappily. She would have go to back to her hotel and phone the hospital from there. Perhaps she'd have more luck if she warned them she was coming. Surely someone must know about Demetri's call.

They had reached the doors when they opened to admit another visitor. The man—security guard?—who was escorting Joanna drew her aside to allow the woman to pass. But, to the surprise of both of them, she stopped.

'Mrs Manning,' she said, her dark eyes widening in surprise. '*Theos*, what are you doing? Where are you going?'

Olivia! Joanna's spirits plummeted still further. Of all the people to see, it had to be Olivia. The person least likely to do anything to help her.

Olivia's greeting had activated a totally different reaction, however. The security guard had now dropped his hand from her arm and the receptionist, who only moments before had been telling Joanna there was nothing she could do, now came fluttering nervously across the marble floor.

'Oh, Kiria Kastro,' she exclaimed, but that was as much as Joanna could understand. The rest was an unintelligible gabble, even if the gist was fairly plain. She was gesturing agitatedly towards Joanna, and she wondered if the girl was blaming her because they'd been on the point of rejecting her. Whatever, as soon as Olivia could get a word in, Joanna had no doubt she'd be on her way again, albeit without an escort this time.

'*Stamateo!* That is enough.' To Joanna's amazement, Olivia stopped the receptionist's tirade with an impatient exclamation. Then, speaking in English for Joanna's benefit, she went on, 'Are you saying you have not informed my brother that Mrs Manning is here?'

'Kiria Kastro—'

'I will take that as a no, shall I?' Olivia had the enviable knack of reducing the most voluble protest to nothing. She glanced about her impatiently, ignoring the imploring gestures the other woman was making. Then, turning to Joanna, 'I am sorry about this, Mrs Manning. I felt sure Demetri would have left instructions for you to be taken up to my father's suite as soon as you arrived.'

Joanna was taken aback. The last thing she'd expected was that Olivia would want her here. 'I—he didn't know I was coming,' she admitted awkwardly. 'I—just booked a ticket and came.'

'*Okhi!*' Olivia was looking concerned now. 'So—you have not spoken to my brother?'

'No.' Joanna didn't understand her agitation. 'Does it matter?'

'It may.' Olivia heaved a sigh. 'If Demetri has already left for the airport.'

Joanna didn't know whether to feel glad or sorry. If Demetri wasn't here, her fears of seeing him again would be removed. She might even be able to return to London without ever exchanging a word with him. It was obvious he'd told Olivia that he'd tried to contact her, which surely proved he felt no guilt over what he'd done. She was just a necessary encumbrance; someone his father had become attached to but who would be quickly forgotten once the old man was dead.

Dead!

Joanna shivered again. Constantine dead. She couldn't bear to think about that.

'Demetri was intending to fly to England this evening.'

Joanna realised Olivia was still speaking, and struggled to comprehend what she was saying. 'To—to England?' she echoed, realising she was making no contribution to this conversation. 'I didn't know that.'

'How could you?' Olivia flicked another disparaging glance at the receptionist. 'But he had apparently tried to reach you by phone without any success.'

Joanna swallowed. 'He was coming to see me?'

'Who else?' Just for a moment a trace of Olivia's usual arrogance coloured her tone. Then, turning to the receptionist again, she said curtly, 'Do you know where Mr Kastro is?'

'Mr Demetri Kastro?' The girl was flustered.

'As I doubt my father is capable of leaving his bed, I have a reasonably good idea where he is,' countered Olivia irritably. '*Ne*, I meant my brother. Is he still here?'

The girl licked her lips. 'I— I—'

'I see you are still terrorising the staff, Livvy,' remarked a dry voice from behind them, and Joanna swung round to find the man she'd told herself she least wanted to see striding towards them from the direction of a bank of lifts. In a dark blue button-down shirt and black pants, his jacket looped casually over one broad shoulder, Demetri was at his most intimidating. His eyes held hers for a brief, yet devastating moment, before moving back to his sister. 'What is going on?'

Joanna blushed. She couldn't help herself. The realisation that the last time she'd been with this man he'd been slumped naked across her quivering body caused a wave of heat to envelop her. God, how was she supposed to deal with this? How was she supposed to deal with him?

Thankfully, Olivia wasn't looking at her. Waving the receptionist back to her desk, she said crisply, 'Just a small misunderstanding, Demetri. As you can see, Mrs Manning is here. But if that stupid girl had had her way she would have been ejected from the building.'

'*Mou Theos*, is this true?' His eyes turned back to Joanna, dark and unreadable now in his tanned face. 'Why did you not return my call? I could have arranged for someone to meet you at the airport.'

'Well—'

'I think Mrs Manning prefers to be independent, Demetri,' Olivia broke in smoothly. 'Besides, I doubt she has your number. Unless you left it for her, of course.'

'She could have reached me via the hospital,' replied Demetri shortly. But then, as if realising he was being far too heavy-handed, he switched his attention back to his sister. 'So, Livvy, am I to understand that you have been defending Mrs Manning's right to see our father?' His lips twisted. 'I am impressed.'

'Save your sarcasm, Demetri.' Olivia wasn't amused. 'Perhaps you should escort our visitor upstairs, *ne*? After all, it is Papa she has come to see. Not us.'

Demetri swung his jacket down from his shoulder and pushed his arms into the sleeves with careless grace. 'Why not?' he conceded, his politeness tinged with bitterness. 'It would seem that my journey is no longer necessary. I must ask Spiro to get on to the airline and cancel my ticket.'

'I will do that,' said Olivia, accompanying them across to the lift. 'Is he at the Athens office?'

'He was an hour ago,' agreed Demetri, pausing to allow Joanna to precede him into the panelled cubicle a uniformed attendant had waiting for them. *'Efharisto!'*

'Efharistisi mou,' responded Olivia drily, and walked away.

CHAPTER FIFTEEN

THE attendant's presence in the lift meant any kind of private conversation was difficult, and Joanna told herself she was glad. She and Demetri had nothing to say to one another. She was here to see his father, as Olivia had said. She should be grateful that his sister had chosen to be civil to her. Without Olivia's intervention she would have found her position impossible, particularly if Demetri had left for London.

'You had a good journey?'

Demetri's enquiry caught her unawares. She had been concentrating on the indicator light as it moved up through the floors. It was with some trepidation that she discovered he had come to rest his shoulder against the wall of the lift beside her, successfully blocking her view of the attendant.

'It—was all right,' she replied, not in the mood to explain that her seat had been over the wing and she'd been nearly deafened by the roar of the engines. 'It was delayed for half an hour.'

Demetri's nostrils flared. 'You should have returned my call,' he said with sudden vehemence. 'I would have arranged your flight.'

'That wasn't necessary.'

'No.' A sardonic expression crossed his face. 'You enjoy thwarting my wishes, Joanna. I was beginning to think that Spiro had given me the wrong number.'

Joanna's head felt light. 'I'm sorry.'

'Are you?' To her consternation, he lifted his hand and traced the line of her jaw with his finger. 'Why do you not look at me, *agapitos*? Are you so ashamed of what we did together?'

Joanna's eyes went wide, and this time she couldn't prevent herself from looking at him. 'You shouldn't say things like that,' she protested, her eyes darting round his broad shoulder to where the attendant was standing gazing at the indicator board. 'I—someone could hear you.'

Demetri lifted a dismissive eyebrow. 'He does not speak English,' he declared indifferently. 'And you did not answer my question.'

Joanna's chest fluttered. 'How—how is your father?' she asked, refusing to play his game. 'I'm looking forward to seeing him again.'

Demetri looked as if he would have liked to continue his baiting, but the mention of his father's name brought him upright from his lounging position. 'He is much better than when we brought him here,' he responded formally. 'He is lucky. His determination to keep us all in the dark could have cost him his life.'

It was a challenging statement and Joanna didn't know how to answer him. 'He— I expect he did not wish to cast a shadow over your sister's wedding celebrations,' she said uneasily, and Demetri gave her a sombre look.

'Let us not pretend that you did not know exactly what he was doing,' he said steadily. 'You were his—co-conspirator; his confidante. But not his mistress, *ne*?'

Joanna's cheeks flamed again. 'Have—have you told your father that you know?' she asked faintly, and now colour deepened his tan.

'What do you think I am?' he demanded in a strangled voice, and now Joanna knew the most ridiculous desire to comfort him.

But she had to be sensible. 'I—I don't know what you are, Demetri,' she said, and before he could respond to this the lift stopped and the doors slid open. 'Is this our floor?'

'It is the floor where my father's suite of rooms is situated,' he agreed, stepping out of the lift with her. Then, after the doors had closed again, he gestured towards a door at the end of the corridor. 'You will find nurses in attendance.' He glanced behind him. 'I will wait in the visitors' sitting room. It is along here. Ask the nurse to ring me when you are ready to leave.'

Joanna took a deep breath. 'All right.'

But she wouldn't. If she had her way she'd spend a little time with Constantine and then go back to her hotel. Until she'd spoken to him she didn't know how long he expected her to stay, but, whatever happened, the less she had to do with Demetri the better.

To her relief, Constantine looked much as he had done when they'd first arrived on Theapolis. He looked pale, of course, and tired, but his eyes were bright and became even brighter when they saw her.

'Joanna!' He lifted his hand to beckon her to him. 'Oh, Joanna, I am so glad to see you.'

'And I you,' said Joanna, her eyes misting with tears. 'I've been so worried about you, Constantine. The bulletins I got from the hospital were so—so impersonal.'

'Here—sit here,' said Constantine eagerly, moving so that she could wedge her hip on the side of his bed. He dismissed the hovering nurse with an impatient command, and then squeezed the hand he had captured when she sat down. 'Why did you not come before?'

'Well—'

'No, do not bother to lie to me, Joanna.' He was watching her closely, his dark eyes so like his son's that for a moment Joanna wondered if he could see right into her soul. 'It was Demetri, was it not? He sent you away.'

'No.' Joanna didn't want to take sides, but she couldn't let him think that Demetri was to blame. 'I—my holiday was over,' she said helplessly. 'I didn't know how long you were going to be in hospital and I had to get back to London.'

Constantine looked sceptical. '*Ne?* Well, have it your own way. I know you are only protecting them. I am sure Olivia had her part to play, too. She was never happy with our relationship.'

Joanna hesitated. 'But you have told them now—'

'I think Demetri guessed,' admitted his father wryly. 'Oh, well, it was nice for a time, to have him envy me.'

'Constantine!'

'You do not believe me?' He studied her suddenly pink face with calculating eyes. 'Joanna, I have seen the way he looks at you. I know he is attracted to you, though he may not know it yet himself.'

'Constantine!'

'What? What?' His eyes narrowed. 'You are not flattered that my son considers you a beautiful woman?'

'He doesn't—' Joanna was flustered. 'That is, I don't think this is the sort of conversation we should he having.'

'Why not?' Constantine's greying brows arched interrogatively. 'Would you rather we discussed this wasted body of mine? Would you rather I told you that the doctors are not sure how much longer I have left?'

'Please—'

'Oh, my dear...' His expression was gentle now. 'Do not upset yourself. I have accepted the situation and so must you. We all die some time. I consider I am fortunate to be given the opportunity to prepare for my death.'

Joanna shook her head. 'I don't know what to say.'

'You could say that you will miss me,' he prompted, lifting her chin with a slightly unsteady hand. 'We have been good friends, you and I. Have we not?'

'You know we have.'

'*Poli kala*, it is natural that I should want to ensure your happiness before it is too late?'

'My happiness?' Joanna stared at him now. Then, as a possible explanation occurred to her, she added swiftly, 'I am happy. I have my work. You know I have a decent place to live. I have friends—'

'That is not what I meant, Joanna.' Constantine regarded her steadily. 'I know you have your work, and, yes, I have seen your apartment and it is as attractive as you can make it. But I want to ensure that if you tire of being at Martin Scott's beck and call you will have the funds to do something else. Whatever you wish.'

Joanna's jaw dropped for a moment. But then, recovering herself, she said firmly, 'No, Constantine.' She took a deep breath. 'I don't want anything from you. Except your friendship. And I believe I already have that.'

Constantine sighed. 'Do not be difficult, Joanna.'

'I am not being difficult.' She didn't want to upset him, but he had to understand that she meant what she said. 'Please, we've discussed this before.'

'Do you remember the day we went to Agios Antonis?' said Constantine obliquely. 'That was a good day, was it not? We went to the jeweller's and I persuaded you to let me buy you a small token—'

'It was hardly a small token,' Joanna interrupted him. 'Even now, I don't think—'

'The bracelet is yours, Joanna.' She could see he was getting agitated now, and she decided not to argue with him. 'I have enjoyed buying things for you, *agapi mou*.' His eyes darkened. 'There is so much more I would like to do, but—'

He broke off then, and Joanna took the opportunity to reassure him. 'You've done everything for me, Constantine,' she said huskily, 'I don't know what I'd have done without you.'

He smiled a little wistfully. 'You are a good girl, Joanna. You have made me realise that I have done things in my life for which I am ashamed. As you know, it was I who encouraged Olivia to marry Andrea Petrou. I knew she was too young, too headstrong, but it was a political coup and that was all that mattered to me. Then, when she told me she wanted a divorce, I was not sympathetic.' He shook his head. 'Do you think she has forgiven me?'

'I'm sure she has,' said Joanna warmly, remembering how concerned Olivia had always been about her father. 'Why don't you ask her?'

'Perhaps I will.' He smiled. 'Perhaps I will. Thank you.'

Joanna stroked the veined back of his hand. 'Just get strong again,' she said gently. 'That's what we all want. Then Demetri can take you home to Theapolis.'

'Ah, Demetri.' Constantine closed his eyes for a moment and Joanna wondered if that was her cue to leave. But before she could act on it he opened them again and said consideringly, 'Tell me, Joanna: what do you really think of my son?'

Joanna was astounded. It was the last thing she had expected him to ask, and she wondered if Demetri had lied to her after all. Had he told his father about their affair? Had Olivia? Did Olivia know?

'Demetri?' she murmured at last, and Constantine gave her a retiring look.

'How many sons do I have, Joanna?' he enquired mildly. 'What is wrong? Do you dislike him that much?'

'No—' She couldn't allow him to think that.

'I thought not.' Constantine's tone was ironic. 'That is not usually the effect he has on your sex.'

Joanna's tongue circled her upper lip. 'He— I— We hardly know one another,' she mumbled, not altogether truthfully, and saw the mocking glint come into Constantine's eyes.

But, 'No,' he conceded, apparently not prepared to pursue it. Instead, he added, 'I told you, did I not, that he and Athenee Sama used to be close friends? Yes? And when she and her father came to Alex's wedding I think both Aristotle and I hoped...' He shrugged. 'But it was not to be.

Something had happened. Demetri had changed. He was no longer interested in Athenee. In fact, he was not interested in any of the young women who flocked around him after the ceremony. Do you know why that should be so, Joanna? Can you explain why a man who has hitherto shown a perfectly natural interest in the opposite sex should suddenly shun even the most innocent of overtures? Can you tell me that?'

Joanna felt hot. 'Have you asked him?' she said, desperately seeking an answer he would accept. She got up from the bed. 'I—perhaps I ought to go. I'm sure your family—'

'Demetri was with you the night I was taken ill, was he not?' Constantine said abruptly, and Joanna couldn't prevent a gasp of dismay. 'Did you honestly think I would not find out?'

Joanna was stunned. 'But—but—'

'How?' suggested Constantine, and she nodded. 'I think you both forgot Philip,' he continued drily. 'He may be old, but his wits are as sharp as ever.'

'Oh, God!' Joanna couldn't look at him. 'And you let me come here knowing—'

'Why not?' Constantine was impatient now. 'We were not lovers, Joanna. I borrowed a little of your time, that is all. You played your part to perfection. How can I be angry with you because my son has allowed his hormones to rule his head?'

She shook her head. 'Does Demetri know?'

'No.' Constantine paused. 'I wanted to tell you first.'

Joanna sighed. 'It wasn't his fault.'

'You would say that, of course.'

'It's the truth.' Joanna was desperate. 'He came to my room to talk. That was all. But, well—one minute we were talking, and the next—'

'Spare me the details,' said Constantine wryly. 'I am sure my son is nothing like your ex-husband.'

'Oh, Constantine…' Joanna pressed her hands to her hot cheeks. Then, remembering, 'But why would Philip tell you something like that? I thought he was your friend.'

'He is.' Constantine gave a twisted smile. 'He thought he was saving me from further heartache. He made a special trip from the island so that he could see me.'

Joanna tried to take it all in. 'And Demetri didn't suspect?'

'Why would he? As far as he and Olivia were concerned Philip was doing what any loyal employee of long standing would do.' Constantine attempted to move his thin shoulders. 'My son has had—other things on his mind.'

'Your illness.' Joanna nodded.

'That, too, of course.' Constantine was looking very tired now, and she realised he had been talking for far too long. 'But—I have noticed a certain restlessness about him, an unexpected desire to get back to the island.' He breathed more shallowly. 'You see,' he persisted, 'until Olivia told him otherwise, he thought you were still there.'

Joanna could only stare at him. 'Constantine...'

But the old man was visibly wilting. 'Not now,' he whispered, his breathing becoming more laboured. 'Later, Joanna. Come back later. Now—I need to—sleep—'

Joanna was waiting for the lift when Demetri came striding along the corridor towards her. His expression revealed his irritation that she had countermanded his instructions, but she was in no mood to care.

'Where are you going?' he demanded, staring at her now pale features with some concern. 'I thought I asked you to let me know when you were leaving. If the nurse had not rung to tell me that my father is resting now I would still have been waiting for your call.'

Joanna didn't want to talk to him now. Concentrating on keeping her voice steady, she said tightly, 'I'm sorry. But I'd prefer to be alone. Do you mind?'

Demetri's dark face tightened with an emotion she couldn't identify. 'Do I have a choice?' he asked tersely. 'At least tell me where you are going.'

Joanna hesitated. 'Does it matter?'

'It might. If I need to get in touch with you,' he replied shortly. 'I suppose you would not agree to me taking you to my father's house in Athens?'

'No.' Joanna knew she was hardly being polite, but she couldn't help it. 'I—er—I have a hotel room.'

'And the hotel's name?'

Realising she had no reason to withhold it, she told him. 'It's a small hotel, not far from the—'

'I have heard of it.' Demetri's tone indicated his opinion of her choice. Then, with a tightening of his jaw, 'You are coming back, *ne*?'

The lift arrived at that moment, and she heard him utter what she assumed was an oath as the attendant held the doors open for her. Joanna had no choice but to step inside, but Demetri detained them.

'You did not answer me,' he reminded her harshly, and Joanna expelled a nervous breath.

'I—probably,' she murmured, supremely conscious of their audience, whether he could understand English or not. 'Um—thank you for letting me visit your father.'

Demetri's mouth thinned. 'You have seen him,' he said flatly. 'Do you think I could have stopped you?'

Joanna managed a small smile. 'You have a point.'

Demetri stepped forward then, startling both her and the attendant by bracing his arms at either side of the lift doors. 'Come back, Joanna,' he said, his voice slightly uneven now. 'For my sake.' He drew a harsh breath. 'If you can forgive me.'

CHAPTER SIXTEEN

JOANNA'S apartment was in north-west London. She'd sold the flat she'd had in Kensington when she and Richard had married. Although it wasn't a particularly fashionable part of the city, the high-rise where she now lived was fairly new, and Demetri had to press the bells of several apartments before someone buzzed him in without querying his identity first.

He'd tried Joanna's apartment, naturally. But she was either out or not answering at the moment, and he wasn't prepared to hang about outside, waiting for her to get home. It was after six already, and November in London was just as chilly as he remembered from his student days. A cold wind probed at his loose cashmere overcoat and he thought ruefully of the more temperate climate of his homeland.

Spiro was waiting in the chauffeur-driven limousine outside, but when Demetri stepped into the carpeted lobby of the building he signalled to his assistant that he could go. He'd contact him on his mobile later, if necessary. And, in the present circumstances, he had to accept that that was

260

likely. Joanna hadn't returned any of his calls, and, although his father's lawyers had received a polite response to their letters, she had refused point-blank to have anything to do with the legacy Constantine had left to her.

That was why he was here, he told himself. Since his father's funeral there had been no contact of any kind between them, and he was growing not only angry but frustrated. Just because she despised him that was no reason to reject his father's last wishes, and he intended to do everything in his power to change her mind.

It was six weeks since he'd buried his father, and this was the first opportunity he'd had to come here. Becoming the head of Kastro International had not been easy. He'd thought he was prepared for the weight of responsibility he would have to shoulder, but the reality had proved so much harder to bear. Apart from anything else, in those first few weeks he had been grieving, too, and he had been astonished by the sense of bereavement he'd felt—not just at his father's death, but at Joanna's refusal to speak to him. It was crazy, he knew, but he'd badly needed some support and she was the only person he'd wanted to give it to him.

Somehow he'd got through the worst of it. And, despite the fact that Constantine had always jealously guarded his position in the company, Demetri had decided it was time for change. In consequence, much to her delight, he had appointed Olivia as his second-in-command, and promoted Nikolas Poros and another of the directors to positions of real authority at last.

Now, with the knowledge that the company wouldn't fall apart in his absence, Demetri was free to do what he wanted for once. Ever since his father's funeral he'd been desperate to speak to Joanna, and, whether she liked it or not, she was going to hear what he had to say.

Of course, he knew she probably wouldn't like him coming here. Despite the fact that she'd maintained a certain civility between them while she was in Athens, her loyalty to his father had made any real conversation stilted. He had no idea if she knew that Constantine had known they were together the night he'd been taken ill, or that his father had forgiven him for it. There was no way he could have broached that during those tense final days at the hospital, and Joanna had always made it plain that she didn't want him turning up at her hotel. She'd been withdrawn, aloof, only seeming to come alive when she was with his father. He had felt she hated him at times, and he hadn't been able to tell her how he was feeling without risking a total breakdown of communication.

She'd left immediately after the funeral, long before Marcos Thexia had gathered the family together for the reading of Constantine's will. And, in his position as the chief beneficiary, Demetri had been obliged to assume his role as head of the family. It had been important that there should be no interruption in the chain of command, and by the time he'd reassured his father's investors, comforted his sisters, and assured his great-uncle that he had no intention of asking him to leave the villa, days had stretched into weeks, heavy with responsibility.

There was a lift, he saw now, with some relief. The thought of climbing to the twelfth floor was rather too much to handle at the moment. Despite—or perhaps because of—the amount of work he'd accomplished, he was weary. He didn't feel as if he'd slept properly since the night his father had been rushed to Athens, and he was exhausted.

Spiro was worried about him, he knew. That was why his assistant had insisted on accompanying him on what was, essentially, a personal visit. He'd made some excuse about Demetri not taking sufficient care of his safety, saying that Olivia thought he should have a handful of bodyguards for his own security, and he was making sure Demetri was protected. But Demetri knew that in truth both Olivia and Spiro supported his decision to come here. Olivia had finally accepted the fact that Joanna was important to him, even if Joanna's behaviour had shown he was clearly not important to her.

Whatever happened, he had to find out why she wouldn't speak to him. He had to do this for his own peace of mind, if nothing else. He wanted to see her. He *needed* to see her. He had to know what, if anything, had happened between them that night at the villa…

Joanna had heard the buzzer while she was clearing out her kitchen cupboards. It had seemed to go on and on, and she guessed it was a salesman, trying his uttermost to get into the building. They did that sometimes. Pressed all the buttons until someone lost patience and let them in. Legitimate visitors usually rang a couple of times and then gave up.

She was surprised, therefore, when in a short space of time someone knocked at her door. A salesman couldn't possibly have canvassed the whole building in less than ten minutes, so she didn't hesitate before stripping off her rubber gloves and going to answer it.

She didn't immediately open the door, of course. Although it was some years since she'd seen Richard, there was always the chance that he'd read about Constantine's death and decided to come and tell her he knew she no longer had a protector. It was a twisted thought, and not one she really gave any credence to. But she hadn't lived alone for several years without becoming cautious.

There was another urgent tattoo as she was putting her eye to the observation hole that all the apartment doors were fitted with, and she almost jumped out of her skin. Impatient devil, she thought, half inclined to pretend she wasn't in after all. But then curiosity got the better of her, and she peered out.

It was Demetri!

She stared at him greedily for several seconds, and then turned to press her shoulders back against the door. Demetri, here, she thought incredulously. Oh, God, she'd imagined she'd finished with the Kastros when she'd written back to their solicitors. She didn't want Constantine's legacy. Even though she might live to regret it, she couldn't put herself in their debt. Particularly not now.

She closed her eyes for a moment, and then opened them again to cast a critical glance over her appearance. Loose-fitting jeans; a cotton sweater with its sleeves rolled up; canvas trainers. With her hair drawn back into a ponytail, it was certainly not the appearance she'd have chosen to present at an interview with Demetri, but perhaps that was just as well. He could hardly accuse her of trying to vamp him in this outfit.

Pulling the sweater out of the tightening waistband of her jeans, she patted it down over her stomach. Then, taking a deep breath and praying she was up to this, she opened the door.

'Demetri,' she said, infusing her voice with just the right amount of cool detachment. Her brows arched. 'What are you doing here?'

His thin smile was forced. 'May I come in?'

No!

'Why not?' She stepped back to allow him into her living room. 'But I think I should warn you that if you've come to try and persuade me to accept any of your father's money you're wasting your time.'

Demetri's lips twisted. 'Just so long as I remember that,' he remarked drily, walking across her oatmeal-coloured carpet. He looked about him with interest. 'This is nice.'

'Thank you.' Joanna closed the door with some reluctance and leaned back against it again. 'I think so.'

Demetri turned, pushing his hands into the pockets of the charcoal-grey overcoat he was wearing. He looked pale, she mused unwillingly, refusing to acknowledge the twinge of anxiety she felt at the thought. Pale, and tired. But still as sinfully attractive as ever.

'How are you?' he asked, and, realising they couldn't continue talking in this stand-off position, Joanna gestured to the sofa behind him.

'Please,' she said, and she guessed it was a measure of his weariness that he didn't wait for her to sit down first before subsiding onto the overstuffed cushions. Then, carelessly she hoped, 'I'm fine.' She paused. 'I expect you're very busy.'

Demetri shrugged. 'We are coping,' he replied, and Joanna guessed that was probably the understatement of the year. If his appearance was anything to go by, he was working himself to death. 'My father is a hard act to follow.'

Joanna thought if anyone could do it he could, but she didn't say that. Instead, she hesitated only a moment before straightening and asking, 'Can I get you anything? Tea? Coffee? A beer?'

'Beer?' Demetri frowned. 'You drink beer?'

She could have said no, that it had been bought for those occasions when Constantine had visited her apartment, but she didn't see why she should explain herself to him.

So, 'Sometimes,' she murmured untruthfully. Then, 'I'm afraid I don't have anything stronger.'

Demetri's eyes were dark and penetrating for a moment, but then his lids dropped and he inclined his head. 'Thank you.'

She went into the kitchen on legs that felt decidedly shaky. Dear heaven, what was she doing, offering him refreshment when she should have been doing her best to get him out of there?

But it was too late now. Taking a beer from the fridge, she collected a glass and returned to the living room. Demetri was still sitting on the sofa, but now he was lying back, his head resting on the cushions, his eyes closed.

Was he asleep? She hovered, not sure what to do, but then he opened his eyes and saw her. '*Signomi*—I am sorry,' he said hastily, pushing himself upright. 'You must forgive me. It has been a long day.'

More than one, thought Joanna, despising herself for caring. It was nothing to do with her if he chose to drive himself so hard he was injuring his health. He was a young man. He'd survive.

Handing over the bottle of beer and the glass, she sought the edge of a nearby chair and perched upon it. 'So, why are you here, Demetri? Are you in London on business?'

He didn't answer her directly. Instead he was looking at the bottle, and a slow smile slid over his face. 'Ah, this used to be my father's favourite,' he said, unscrewing the cap. His brows arched interrogatively. 'Is it your favourite too?'

Joanna sighed and gave in. 'I bought it for him,' she admitted, feeling the pang of loss she always experienced when she thought of Constantine these days. 'He used to come here occasionally. I once made him supper.' She grimaced. 'It wasn't very impressive, but he seemed to enjoy it.'

'I am sure he did.' She decided his response was more rueful than patronising. Then, suddenly realising she wasn't drinking, 'Will you not join me?'

Joanna shook her head. 'I—I'm not a great lover of beer,' she said, wishing she'd thought to bring herself some orange juice, just to give her something to do with her hands. 'Um—you didn't say why you wanted to see me.'

Demetri looked at the beer and the glass, and then set the latter down on the occasional table in front of the sofa. Raising the bottle to his lips, he swallowed at least half its contents in one gulp. Then, savouring its tangy flavour, he wiped his mouth with the back of his hand and looked at her.

'Why did you not answer any of my calls?' he asked at last, when she was wilting beneath his gaze. 'Do you not think you owed me that?'

Joanna moved her head in an awkward little gesture. 'I don't know what you mean.'

'Oh, I think you do.' He put the beer aside and moved to the edge of the sofa. Spreading his legs, he rested his forearms on his thighs. 'Were you afraid? Is that it? Has your experience with your ex-husband made you wary of getting involved with another man?'

'We weren't involved.' Joanna was defensive.

'No?' Demetri regarded her impatiently. 'You are not going to try and tell me you are in the habit of asking a man to make love to you?' he queried drily. 'I was there, Joanna. I know you had never been with a man before.'

'So?' Joanna got up now, unable to sit still under his scrutiny. 'The fact that we had sex together doesn't give you the right to—'

'We did not have sex together,' retorted Demetri harshly, getting to his feet. 'We made love. There is a difference. As you would know, if you were not trying so hard to hate my guts.'

'I don't hate you.' Joanna folded her arms across her midriff. 'I just think you're attaching too much importance to—to something that—that had to happen one day.'

Demetri's mouth turned down. 'So prosaic,' he said wryly. 'So practical.' His lips twisted. 'If I did not know better, I might even be tempted to believe you.'

'Believe it,' urged Joanna, her nervous hands now groping for the hem of her sweater and tugging it down again. 'I—I wish you would.'

Demetri subjected her to another prolonged stare. And then, when she was on the verge of making a panicked retreat into the kitchen, he closed the space between them and cupped the side of her neck with his hand.

'So,' he said, watching her reaction with narrowed eyes. 'If I were to do this—' His fingers tightened and she felt her own pulse beating against his hand. 'Or this—' He bent his head and bestowed a light kiss at the corner of her mouth. 'You would not object?'

Joanna trembled. 'Wh—why would you want to kiss me?' she asked, determined not to let him see how shaken she was by his behaviour. 'Have you exhausted all the women in Greece?'

He swore then, but he didn't let her go, and she swayed a little unsteadily under his hands. 'You are deliberately trying to provoke me,' he said, pulling her hair loose of the elastic tie she'd used to control it and sliding his fingers into its tumbled softness. 'But you are wasting your time. I will not let you drive me away.'

Joanna tried to remain calm. 'I—I just don't know why you've come here,' she protested. 'I know you probably think I'm ungrateful for not wanting your father's money, but I tried to tell him—'

'Forget the money,' said Demetri, drawing her even closer and nuzzling her neck with his lips. '*Theos*, you have no idea how much I have missed you. It is crazy, no? But I have.'

'Demetri—'

'What?' He lifted his head to look down at her with dark soulful eyes. 'You do not believe me? Well...' he rubbed his thumb over her lower lip '...what was it you said? Believe it? Yes, believe it, Joanna. That is why I am here. Because I find I need you in my life.'

Joanna's jaw dropped. 'You don't mean this—'

'Why not?' Demetri's thumb tipped her face up to his now, making it easy for him to brush her mouth with his. 'You cannot deny that from the minute we met there was an irresistible attraction between us.'

'No—'

'Oh, yes.' He was positive. 'You know it is true. The wonder of it is that I kept my hands off you as long as I did.'

Joanna shook her head. 'You've made a mistake.'

'Really?' He didn't sound convinced. 'So you are not attracted to me at all? When I do this…' He stroked a sensual finger down her spine that had her arching helplessly against him. 'Or this…' His free hand slid beneath the hem of her sweater to spread its cool strength against her waist. 'You feel no answering response?'

'I—didn't say I wasn't attracted to you,' she exclaimed breathlessly.

'Then—?'

'I won't be your mistress, Demetri!'

He let her go then, as she'd known he would. A numbing silence followed her outburst and, unable to stand the anti-climax, Joanna backed away towards the door.

'I think you'd better go now,' she added, groping for the handle. 'It was—good of you to come, and—and I am flattered that you find me att—'

'*Skaseh!*'

She didn't recognise the word he used, but its meaning seemed fairly obvious—particularly as it was accompanied by a chopping motion of his hand. His face was dark and ominous, and although his features were still drawn with fatigue, a hectic colour had overlaid his pale cheeks. With a muffled oath, he strode towards her, and she had no time to fumble the door open before he slammed angry hands on the panels at either side of her head.

He stared down at her, his eyes searching her face as if seeking answers she couldn't give. Then, with a savage intensity, he said, 'Did I ask you to be my mistress?'

'No.' Joanna couldn't accuse him of that exactly. 'But you're not going to pretend you didn't come here expecting to—to repeat what happened before?'

'What happened before,' he echoed a little mockingly. 'Oh, Joanna, you have a great deal of trouble in saying what you really mean. Of course I came here because I want to sleep with you. But our relationship does not only consist of what we do in bed.'

'We don't have a relationship!' exclaimed Joanna fiercely. 'You want me. You may even believe you want to make love with me. But at the end of the day—'

'At the end of the day, you do not know what the hell you are talking about,' he told her harshly. 'You do not know how many nights I have lain awake, wondering how I was going to function the next day, never mind take responsibility for an organisation my father was reckless enough to put into my hands—'

'Your father was never reckless,' protested Joanna, grateful for something to say that wouldn't engender any more of his anger. But Demetri wouldn't let her go on.

'My father was reckless,' he contradicted her unsteadily. 'He brought you to Theapolis. He introduced me to the one woman I thought I could never have and then pushed us into one another's company, expecting—' But there he broke off, shaking his head. '*Theos*, I do not know what he expected any more. All I do know is that my life has not been the same since you came into it. How can you tell me I do not know what I want?'

Joanna trembled. She ought to stop him. She had to stop him. There were things she had to say to him. But all she managed was, 'What do you want, Demetri?' and with a groan he lowered himself against her.

'You,' he said simply, and in a kind of delirium she felt his mouth open over hers. 'You,' he said again, against her lips. 'I love you, *agapitos*. And I have never said that to any woman.'

Joanna's head swam at the first taste of his tongue in her mouth. She hadn't realised how much she wanted him to touch her until she'd felt the muscled length of his hard body imprisoning her against the door. She hadn't known her breasts had become so sensitive, or bargained for the melting softness in her lower limbs that was only accentuated when he eased his thigh between her legs. The pulsing heat of his arousal stirred against her stomach, and, giving in to the delicious weakness that was enveloping her, she wound her fingers into his hair.

Demetri's kiss lengthened, deepened, robbed her of her breath. Shrugging off his overcoat, he allowed it to fall to the floor at their feet as he drew her across to the sofa and pulled her down on top of him.

'I have dreamed about this, about you,' he said huskily, his hand behind her head, holding her to him. 'But always before I was in control. Sex was just a game to be played, and I played it like everybody else.' He gave a groan. 'No longer.' His fingers slid beneath her sweater, splaying across her back. 'Now I cannot think of life without you. How controlling is that?'

Joanna drew a quivering breath. 'I can't believe this.'

'What?' He rolled over with her so that now she was crushed beneath him, her heart fluttering wildly in her chest. 'What part of this do you not believe? The fact that I have been nearly out of my head because I could not get away from Athens any sooner? Or that I am in love with you; have been in love with you, I think, since your first morning at the villa. You came out onto the terrace and I watched you from the pool. Oh, yes.' This as her eyes went wide with surprise. 'I watched you for quite some time before I chose to make my presence known.'

'Your nude presence,' murmured Joanna daringly, and was rewarded with a rueful smile.

'My nude presence,' he conceded. 'You noticed.'

'How could I not?' she countered, her courage growing. 'You were—well, you know what you were better than me.'

'Aroused,' he admitted huskily. 'You do that to me.' He took one of her hands and drew it down between their bodies. 'Like this, hmm?'

Joanna's cheeks went pink. 'Demetri, I—'

'Do not say anything,' he advised her gently. 'And you need not be alarmed. I do not intend to do anything to frighten you.'

Joanna brought her hands up to his face. 'You don't frighten me, darling,' she whispered, her thumbs brushing his lips now. 'I love you.' She paused. 'But I think you know that already. Isn't that why you're here?'

'I am here because I want to ask you to marry me,' declared Demetri fiercely, pushing himself up and looking down at her with impassioned eyes. 'I do not want a mistress, Joanna. I want a wife. But not just any wife. You. Only you.'

EPILOGUE

'MY FATHER knew about us,' Demetri murmured some time later, drawing Joanna's naked body into the curve of his. Although he had already made love to her he was still half aroused, and she shifted in unknowing provocation as his erection nudged the sensual cleft of her buttocks.

'I know,' she breathed softly, but he sensed a certain ambivalence in the words and wondered if she still doubted the sincerity of his actions.

But surely she believed that he loved her. *Theos*, he couldn't imagine life without her. Hearing that she loved him had been like having a great weight lifted from him. When he'd carried her into her bedroom and stripped the bulky jeans and sweater from her he'd been sure that nothing and no one could harm them. Yet now he could feel an unsettling barrier between them.

But why?

'He told you?' he ventured now, praying it wasn't his father who was his rival. A living man he could deal with. A ghost? That was something else.

'Mmm,' she conceded, heartening him somewhat when she turned her lips against the arm that was cradling her head. 'Philip came to see him. But I suppose you know that?'

'I did hear something about it,' he admitted wryly. 'I would like to say he gave us his blessing, but I would not go as far as that.'

He sensed rather than saw her smile. 'Do you mean Philip or your father?'

'My father,' Demetri assured her firmly. 'He warned me not to hurt you.'

She tensed then. He felt it. And, needing to see her face, he moved so that she rolled onto her back beside him. In the lamplight she was so beautiful, he thought achingly. Her lips bruised from his kisses, her cheeks pink with a mixture of shyness and—what? Apprehension? Surely not.

'He loved you, you know,' he added huskily, needing to reassure her. 'But I am sure you know that.' His hand sought the swollen fullness of her breast that was tantalisingly close to his chest, his thumb massaging the taut nipple. 'He swore he would come back to haunt me if I let you down.'

'And is that why you're here?' she asked abruptly, startling him by the sudden catch in her tone, and he blew out a defensive breath.

'Say what?'

She shifted again, and his hand, which had slipped caressingly over her abdomen, halted at the triangle of moist curls between her legs. 'I asked—' Her eyes were wide and troubled. 'I asked, is that why you're here? Because of what your father said? Because he gave you the impression that I needed—someone.'

Demetri propped himself up on his elbow now, staring down at her with dark, disbelieving eyes. 'Is that what you think?' He made an expressive gesture. 'Is that why you're acting like you wished this had never happened?'

Joanna's face was indignant now. 'I'm not acting like that,' she protested. 'But—but I don't want you to feel that you're responsible for me.'

'*Khristo!*' Demetri swore. '*Theos*, Joanna, I thought we knew one another better than that.'

She looked a little less anxious now. 'Do you mean that?'

'Of course I mean it.' He bent to bestow a sensuous kiss on the curve of her shoulder. 'I love you, Joanna. Me. Not my father. I am crazy about you. How could you even imagine that anything my father said could influence my feelings?'

She shook her head, but one hand came to stroke his cheek. 'I didn't want you to think—oh, you know what I'm trying to say. What with

Constantine making me a beneficiary in his will and all—'

'Hey, I had forgotten that,' murmured Demetri teasingly. 'But it does prove my point. Why should I feel responsible for a woman who is prepared to turn down a yearly legacy of—?'

'Shh.' She put her fingers over his lips and he opened his mouth to bite them instead. 'Don't say any more,' she exclaimed. 'I believe you.'

'In any case, if anyone has a complaint here, it is I,' Demetri continued drily, smiling as his probing fingers caused her to catch her breath. She was wet and he was instantly aware of his own hard response. 'I have tried to contact you numerous times since you left the island, but you have persistently ignored my calls.'

Joanna drew her upper lip between her teeth. 'Actually,' she said carefully, 'you didn't try to contact me for several weeks. You may have rung me in the last three weeks, but in the beginning you left contacting me to your father's solicitor.'

Demetri sighed. 'All right. I admit that in the days—*weeks*—following my father's funeral I had little time for myself. Nonetheless, if you had contacted me, assuredly I would have returned your call.'

'Would you?'

'Do you doubt it?'

'N—o.'

'Then?' He shook his head. 'Surely you can understand what it was like? I was inundated with people who required my decision about this, my signature on that. I wanted to speak to you. Dear heaven, I wanted to *see* you. But my life was not my own.'

She nodded. 'I understand.'

'Do you?'

'I think so.'

'So—why did you not return my calls?' persisted Demetri, stroking her gently. He looked down at her a little pensively. 'Do you know, I think you have put on a little weight?' He smiled. 'It suits you.'

'That's good.' Joanna drew a breath. 'Because there's a reason for that, too.'

Demetri frowned. 'Too?'

'I—wanted to get in touch with you,' she confessed huskily. 'But—it was difficult.'

'Difficult?'

'I'm pregnant,' she said hurriedly. 'Now do you see why I didn't return your calls?'

Demetri stared at her, feeling as if his breath was trapped somewhere in the back of his throat. 'Pregnant?' he echoed incredulously. 'You are pregnant?'

'Yes.' She licked her lips. 'You're not too shocked are you?'

Demetri didn't know how he felt. Shocked, certainly. Exhilarated, amazingly. But mostly relieved. So relieved. He'd thought for a moment that there was something wrong.

'I cannot believe it,' he said, staring at her helplessly. His eyes strayed to her breasts, still swollen from his lovemaking, to the gentle swell of her stomach, now so understandably rounded. She was expecting his child.

'But you don't mind?' she probed anxiously. 'I mean, I know it's not what you expected—'

'Oh, Joanna!' He suddenly realised how his dazed expression must appear to her. '*Agapi mou*, you have—stunned me, that is all.' He lowered his head and kissed her mouth, his tongue lingering against her lips. 'But as for—what was it you said? Do I mind, no?' He lifted her hand and brought it to his lips. 'My darling, I am overwhelmed, humbled. But—' His brows drew together. 'It is I who should be asking you that question.' He hesitated. 'Perhaps you did not want to tell me.'

Joanna's laughter was tremulous. 'You have to be joking,' she exclaimed, cupping his face between her palms. 'You don't know this, but I've practically spring-cleaned this apartment from one end to the other. Anything to avoid thinking about what I was going to do, what I *could* do. Of course I wanted to tell you. But I didn't know what you'd say, how you'd feel. The last thing I wanted was for you to think that I expected you to marry me because I was having a baby—'

Demetri turned his mouth against her palm. 'Believe me, *agapitos*, it would have been no hardship,' he told her softly. 'As I said before, I have wanted you for what seems like for ever. And now you are mine.' He knew he sounded smug, but he couldn't help it. 'I am content.'

'Olivia may not be so pleased,' murmured Joanna doubtfully, but Demetri only laughed.

'Olivia will not have time to object,' he said wryly. 'As you know, she has always wanted to be involved in the company. Well, now she is. I have made her my deputy. Which means...' He nuzzled her throat. 'We will have all the time in the world to ourselves.'

'But—'

'But nothing,' he insisted, easing his thigh between hers. 'You may be surprised to hear that Olivia encouraged me to come and see you.'

'No—'

'Yes.' He was very certain. 'She has been worried about me. She and Alex both. Unlike you, I have lost weight, and Olivia has finally realised that I need you in my life.' His eyes teased her. 'Does that reassure you?'

'Some,' she admitted, sliding her arms round his neck. Then, 'I suppose I should offer you something to eat, shouldn't I?' Her lips tilted. 'But first—'

Demetri hesitated. 'And—the baby—?'

'Is perfectly content that his daddy is here,' Joanna assured him gently. 'Make love to me, Demetri.' She smiled. 'You see, you have taught me what making love means...'

MILLS & BOON® PUBLISH EIGHT LARGE PRINT TITLES A MONTH. THESE ARE THE EIGHT TITLES FOR JANUARY 2003

A PASSIONATE SURRENDER
Helen Bianchin

THE HEIRESS BRIDE
Lynne Graham

HIS VIRGIN MISTRESS
Anne Mather

TO MARRY McALLISTER
Carole Mortimer

MISTAKEN MISTRESS
Margaret Way

THE BEDROOM ASSIGNMENT
Sophie Weston

THE PREGNANCY BOND
Lucy Gordon

A ROYAL PROPOSITION
Marion Lennox

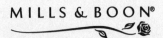

MILLS & BOON®

1202 Rom LP